Mighty Mighty **MONSTERS**

THE GREMLIN'S CURSE

STONE ARCH BOOKS

a capstone imprint

Mighty Mighty Monsters are published by
Stone Arch Books, A Capstone Imprint
1710 Roe Crest Drive
North Mankato, Minnesota 56003
www.capstonepub.com

Cataloging-in-Publication Data is available
at the Library of Congress website.

ISBN: 978-1-4342-3894-8 (library binding)
ISBN: 978-1-4342-4228-0 (paperback)
ISBN: 978-1-4342-4651-6 (eBook)

Summary: Vlad the usually unflappable
vampire is having a really bad day -- so bad
that he begins to wonder if he's cursed!
The Mighty, Mighty Monsters try to help
him out, but they seem to only add to
Vlad's bad luck. But when the gang spots
a new gremlin following Vlad around, they
begin to wonder if the little imp has cast
a bad luck curse on their friend.

Printed in the United States of America in
Stevens Point, Wisconsin.
032012
006678WZF12

Mighty Mighty MONSTERS

THE GREMLIN'S CURSE

created by
Sean O'Reilly

illustrated by
Arcana Studio

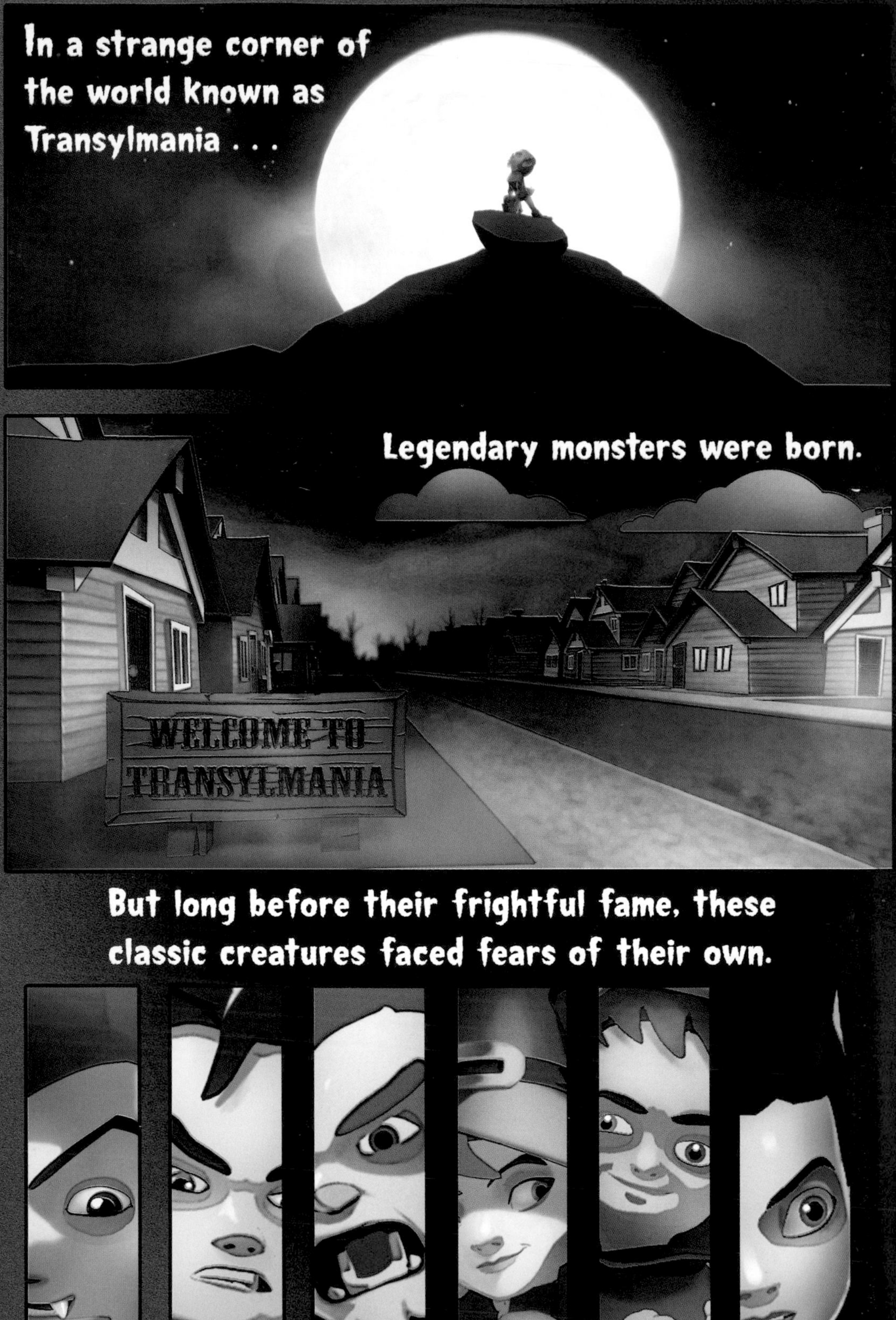
In a strange corner of the world known as Transylmania . . .
Legendary monsters were born.
WELCOME TO TRANSYLMANIA
But long before their frightful fame, these classic creatures faced fears of their own.

To take on terrifying teachers and homework horrors,
they formed the most fearsome friendship on Earth . . .

Mighty Mighty MONSTERS

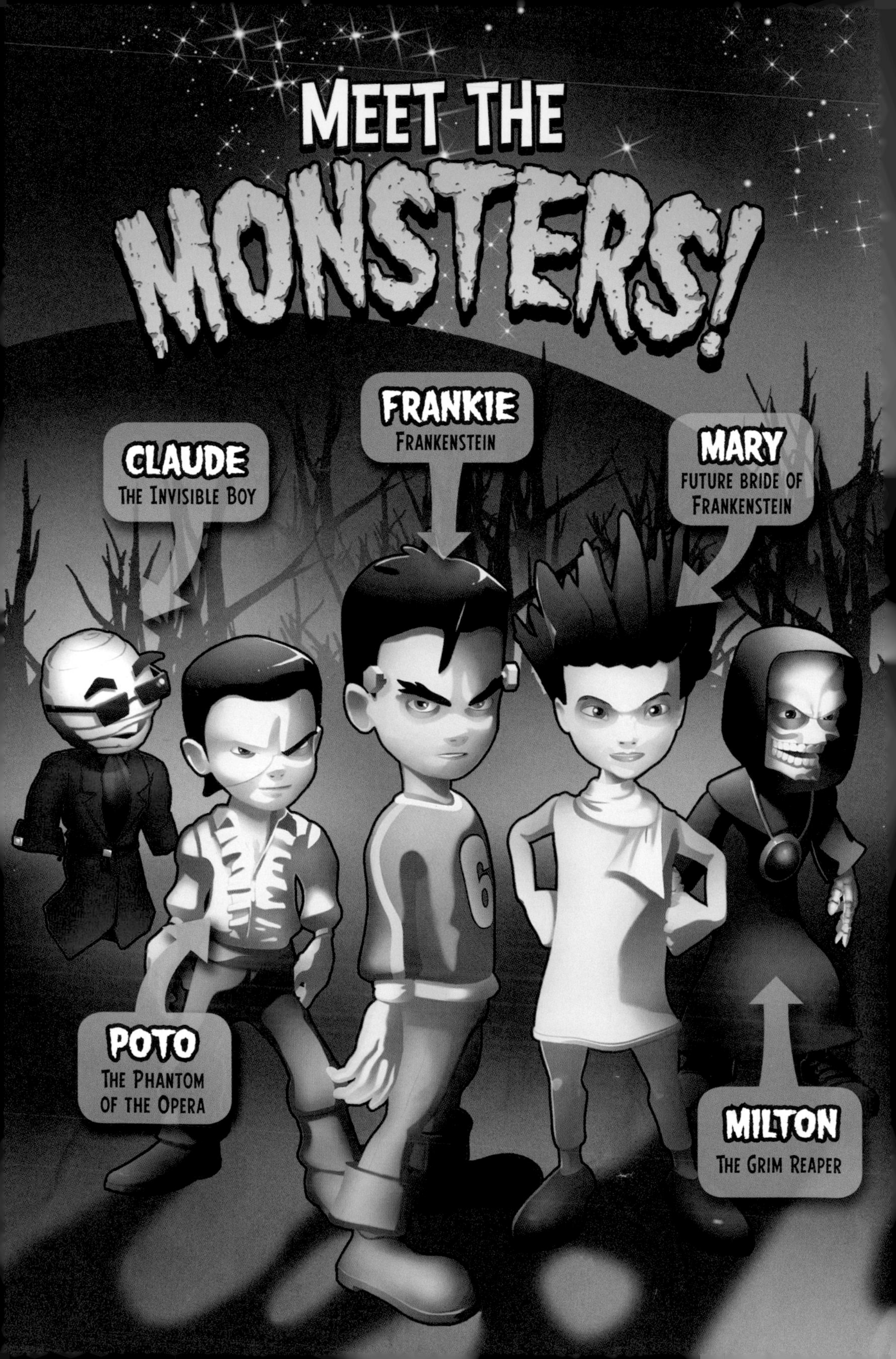
MEET THE
MONSTERS!
CLAUDE
THE INVISIBLE BOY
FRANKIE
FRANKENSTEIN
MARY
FUTURE BRIDE OF
FRANKENSTEIN
POTO
THE PHANTOM
OF THE OPERA
MILTON
THE GRIM REAPER

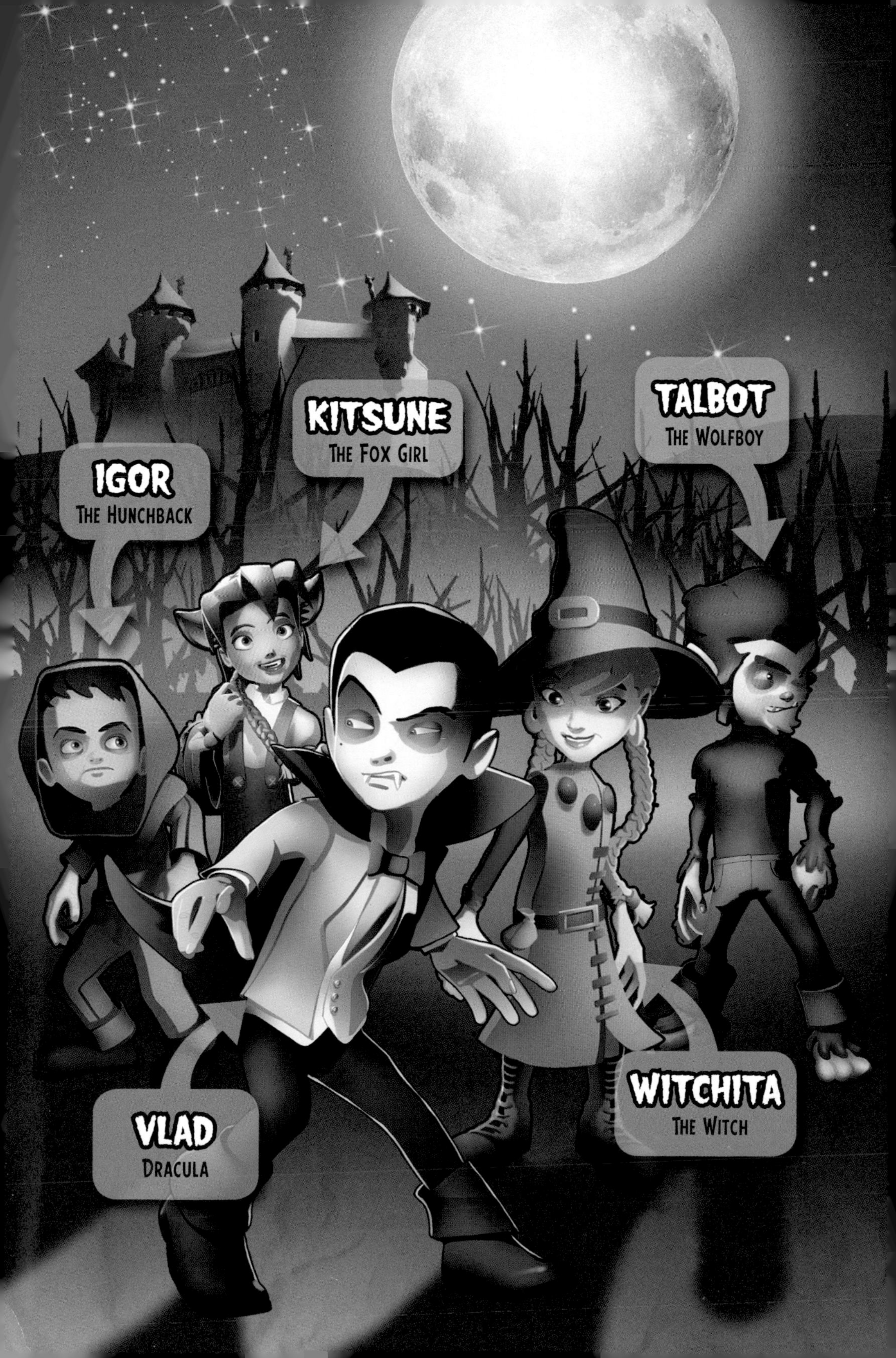
KITSUNE
THE FOX GIRL
TALBOT
THE WOLFBOY
IGOR
THE HUNCHBACK
VLAD
DRACULA
WITCHITA
THE WITCH

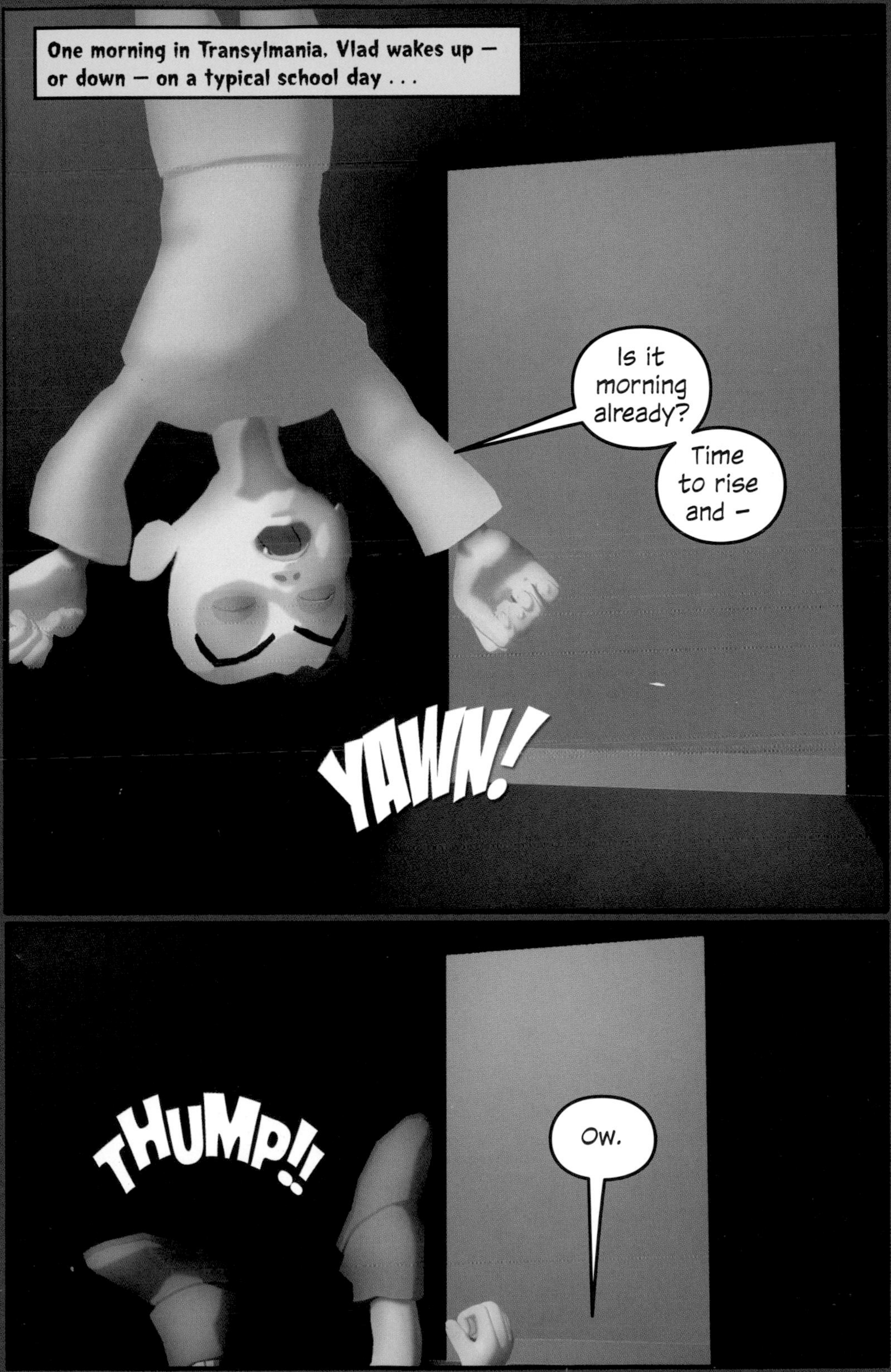

One morning in Transylmania, Vlad wakes up — or down — on a typical school day . . .
Is it morning already?
Time to rise and –
YAWN!
THUMP!!
Ow.

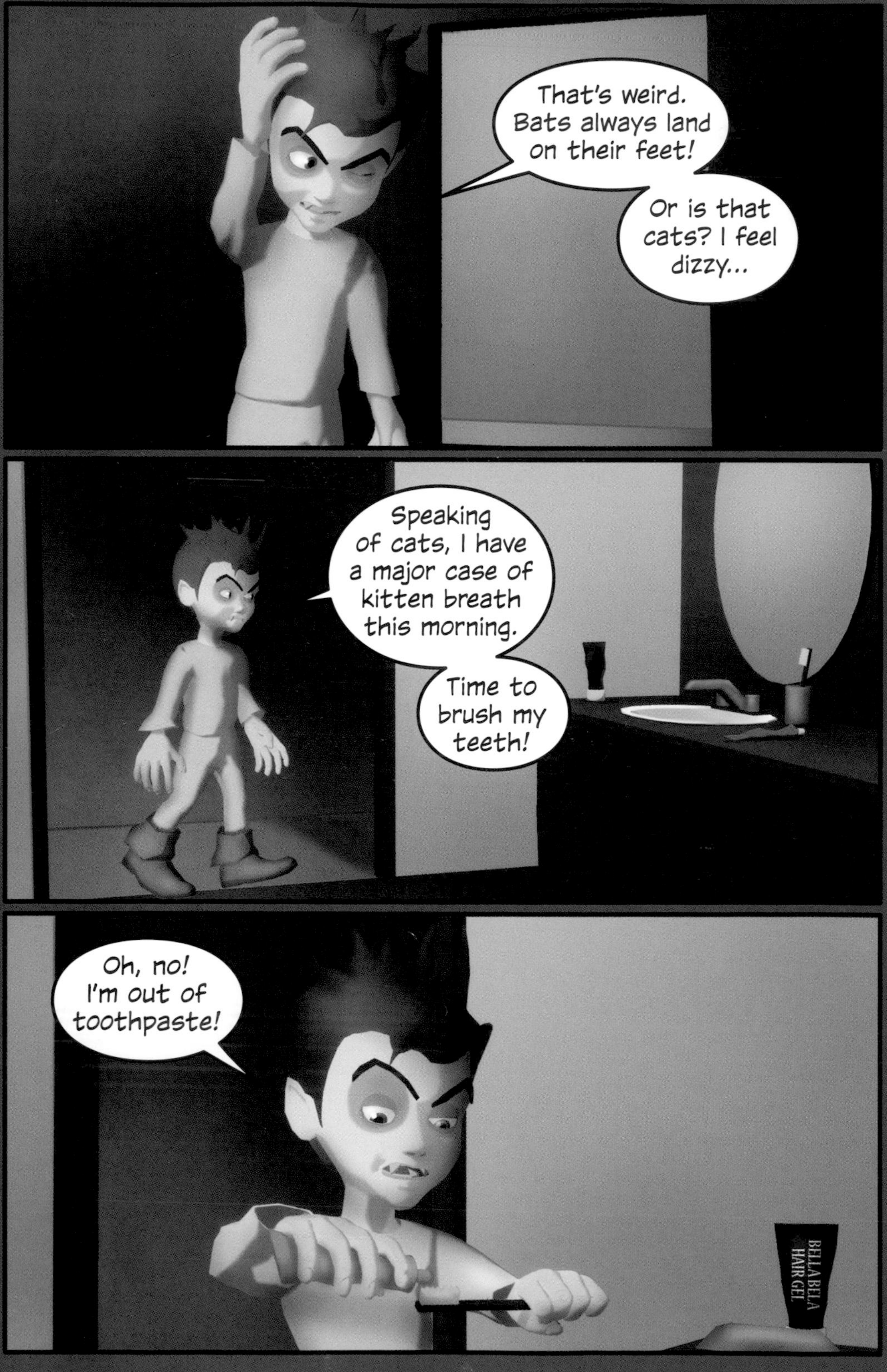
That's weird. Bats always land on their feet!
Or is that cats? I feel dizzy...
Speaking of cats, I have a major case of kitten breath this morning.
Time to brush my teeth!
Oh, no! I'm out of toothpaste!
BELLA BELA
HAIR GEL

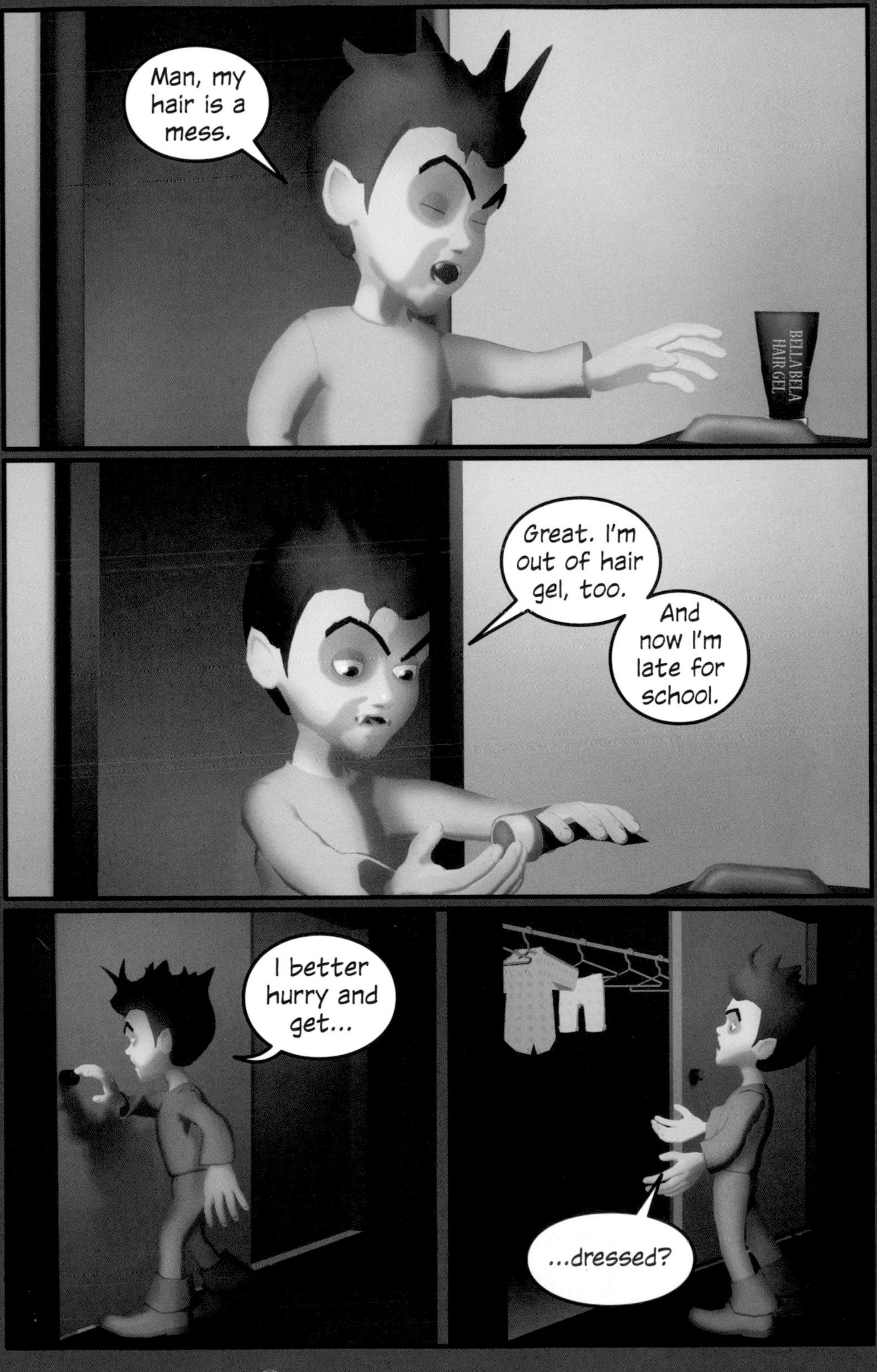
Man, my hair is a mess.
BELLA BELA HAIR GEL
Great. I'm out of hair gel, too.
And now I'm late for school.
I better hurry and get...
...dressed?

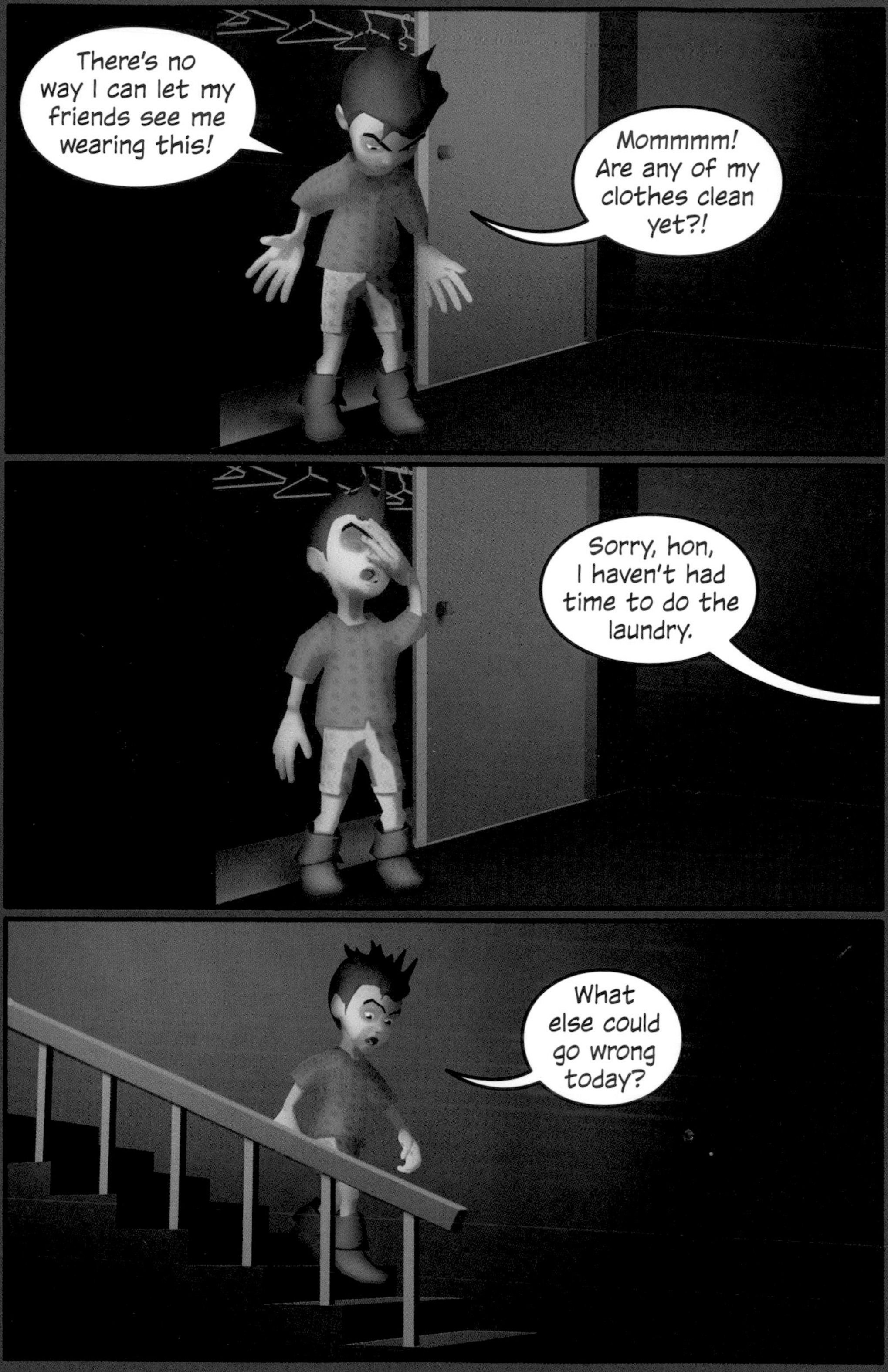
There's no way I can let my friends see me wearing this!
Mommmm! Are any of my clothes clean yet?!
Sorry, hon, I haven't had time to do the laundry.
What else could go wrong today?

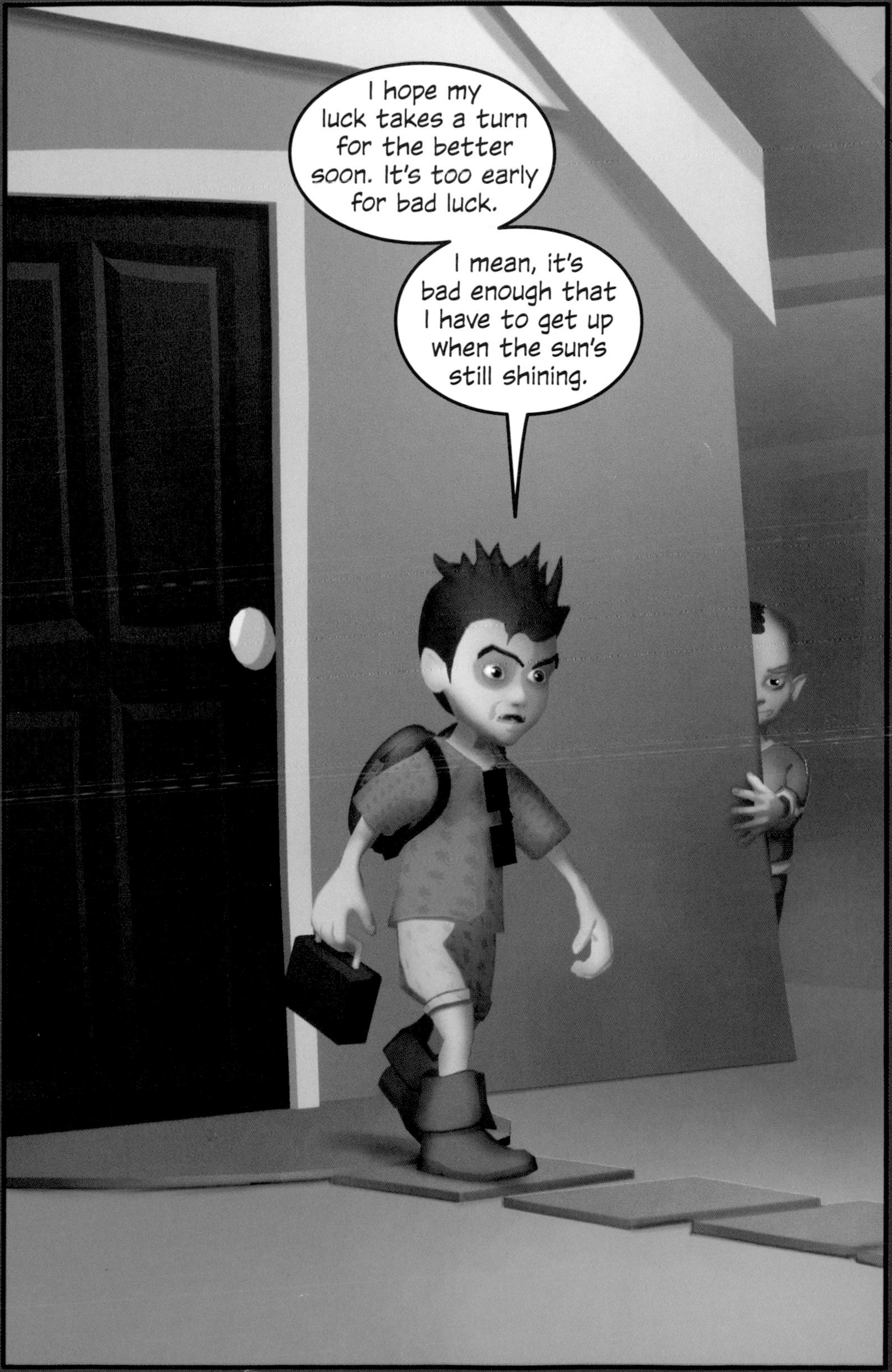
I hope my luck takes a turn for the better soon. It's too early for bad luck.
I mean, it's bad enough that I have to get up when the sun's still shining.

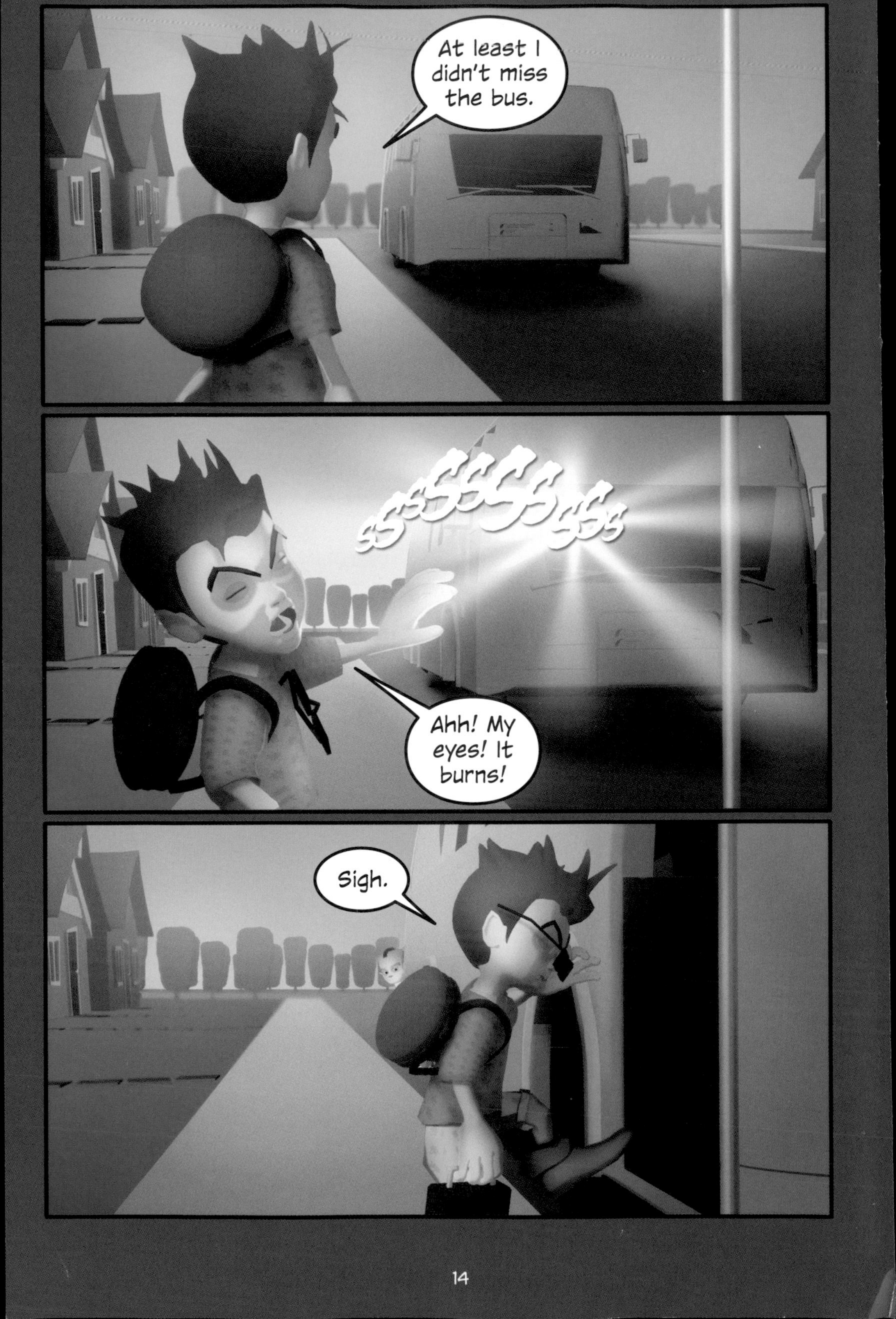
At least I didn't miss the bus.
sSssSSSSsSs
Ahh! My eyes! It burns!
Sigh.

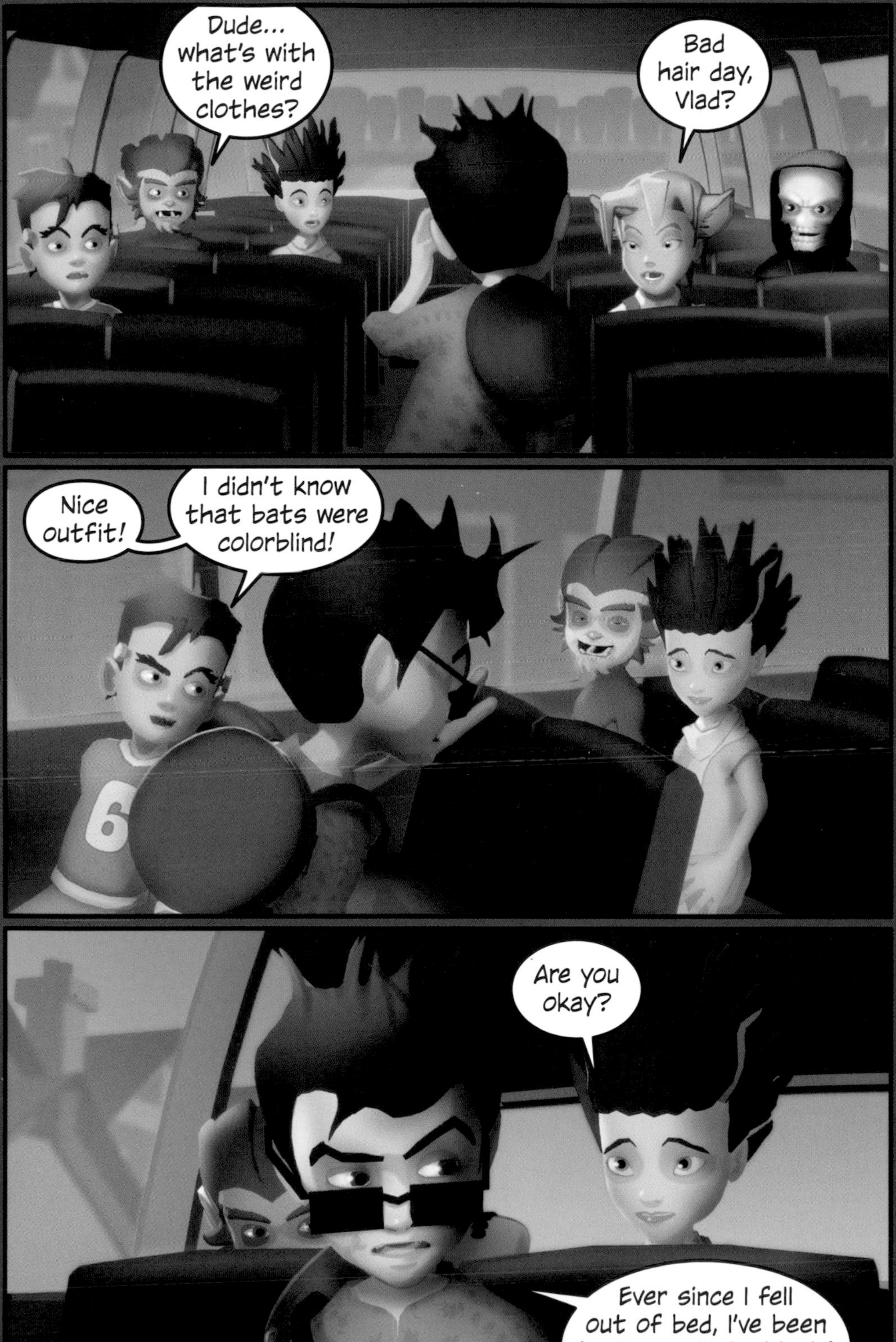
Dude... what's with the weird clothes?
Bad hair day, Vlad?
Nice outfit!
I didn't know that bats were colorblind!
Are you okay?
Ever since I fell out of bed, I've been having really bad luck!

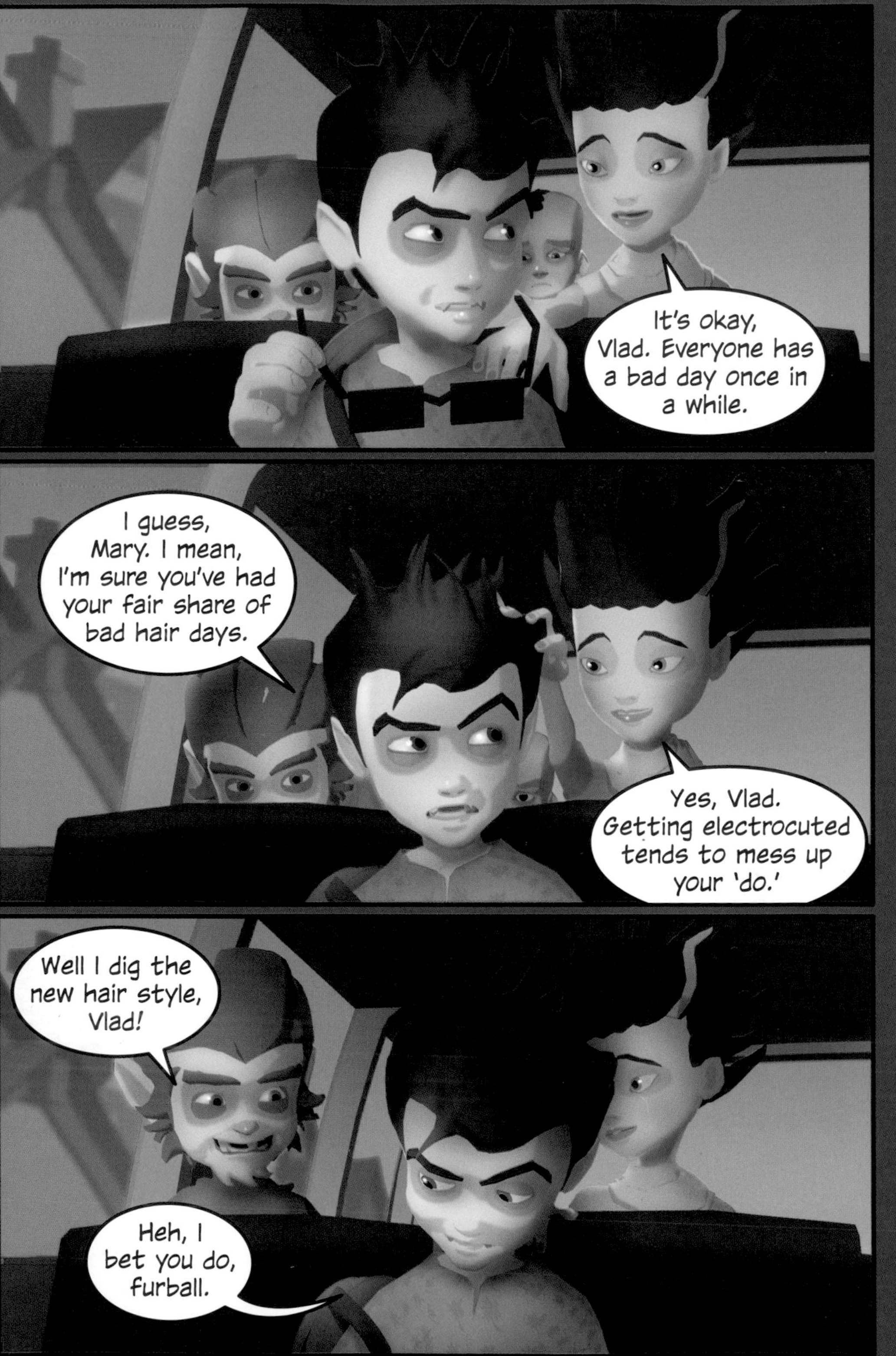
It's okay, Vlad. Everyone has a bad day once in a while.
I guess, Mary. I mean, I'm sure you've had your fair share of bad hair days.
Yes, Vlad. Getting electrocuted tends to mess up your 'do.'
Well I dig the new hair style, Vlad!
Heh, I bet you do, furball.

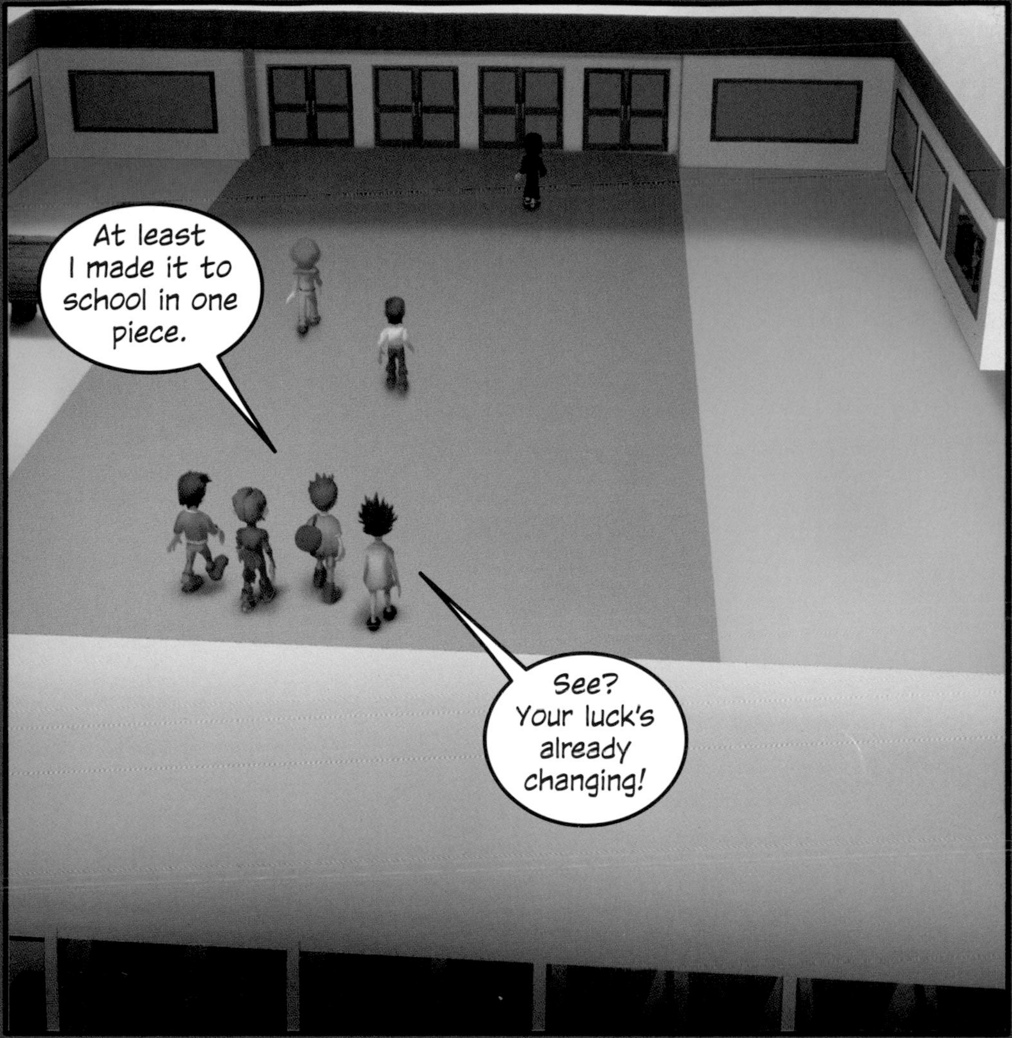
At least I made it to school in one piece.
See? Your luck's already changing!

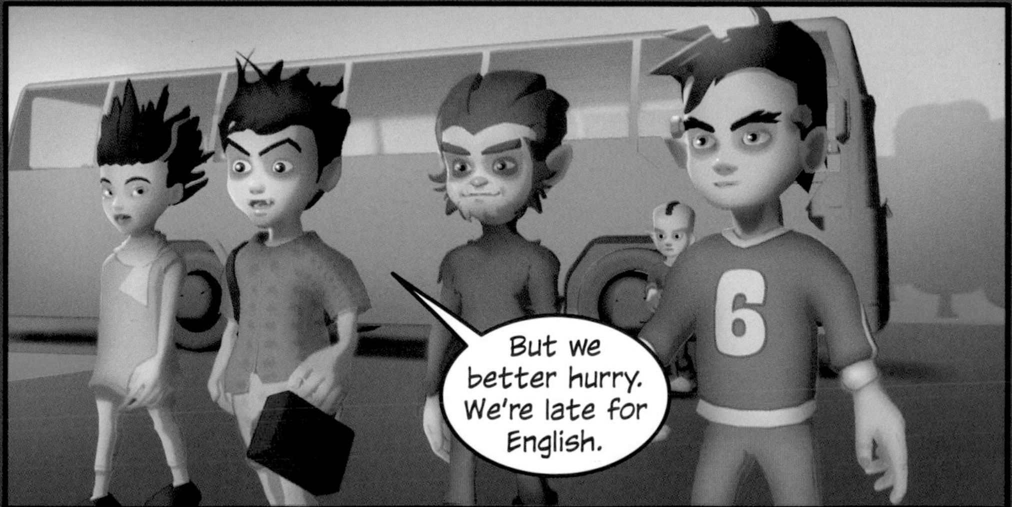
But we better hurry. We're late for English.

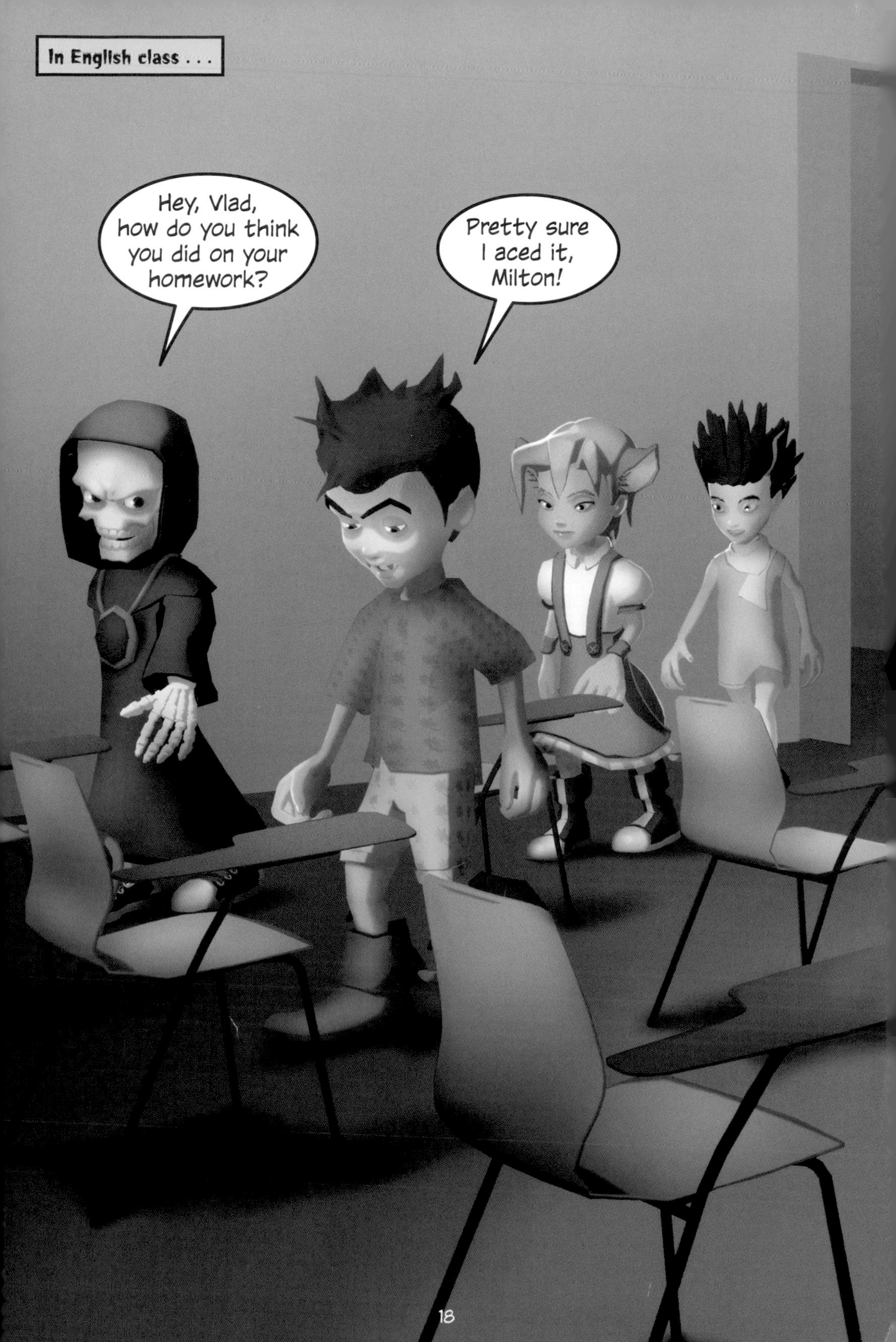
In English class . . .
Hey, Vlad, how do you think you did on your homework?
Pretty sure I aced it, Milton!

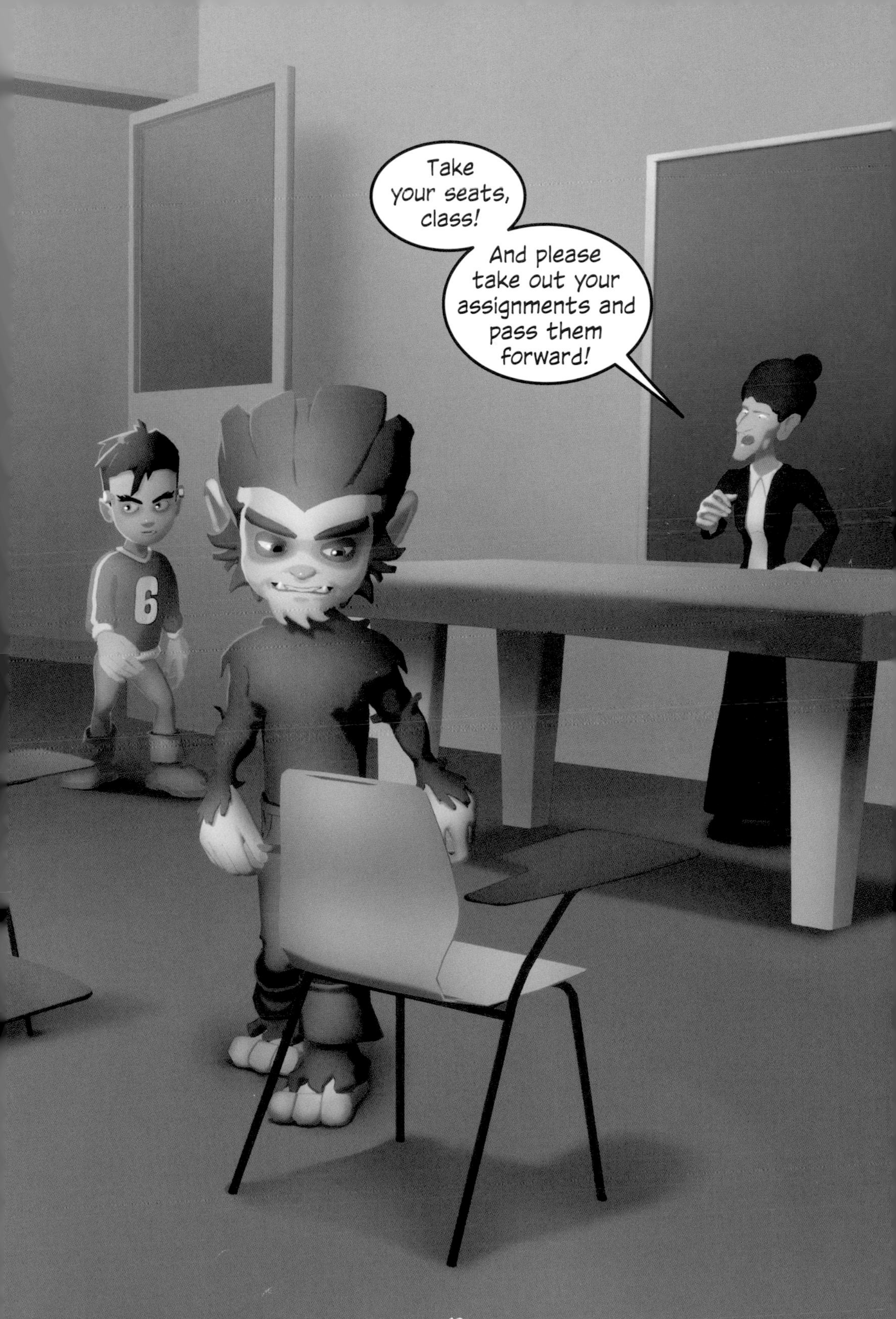
Take your seats, class!
And please take out your assignments and pass them forward!

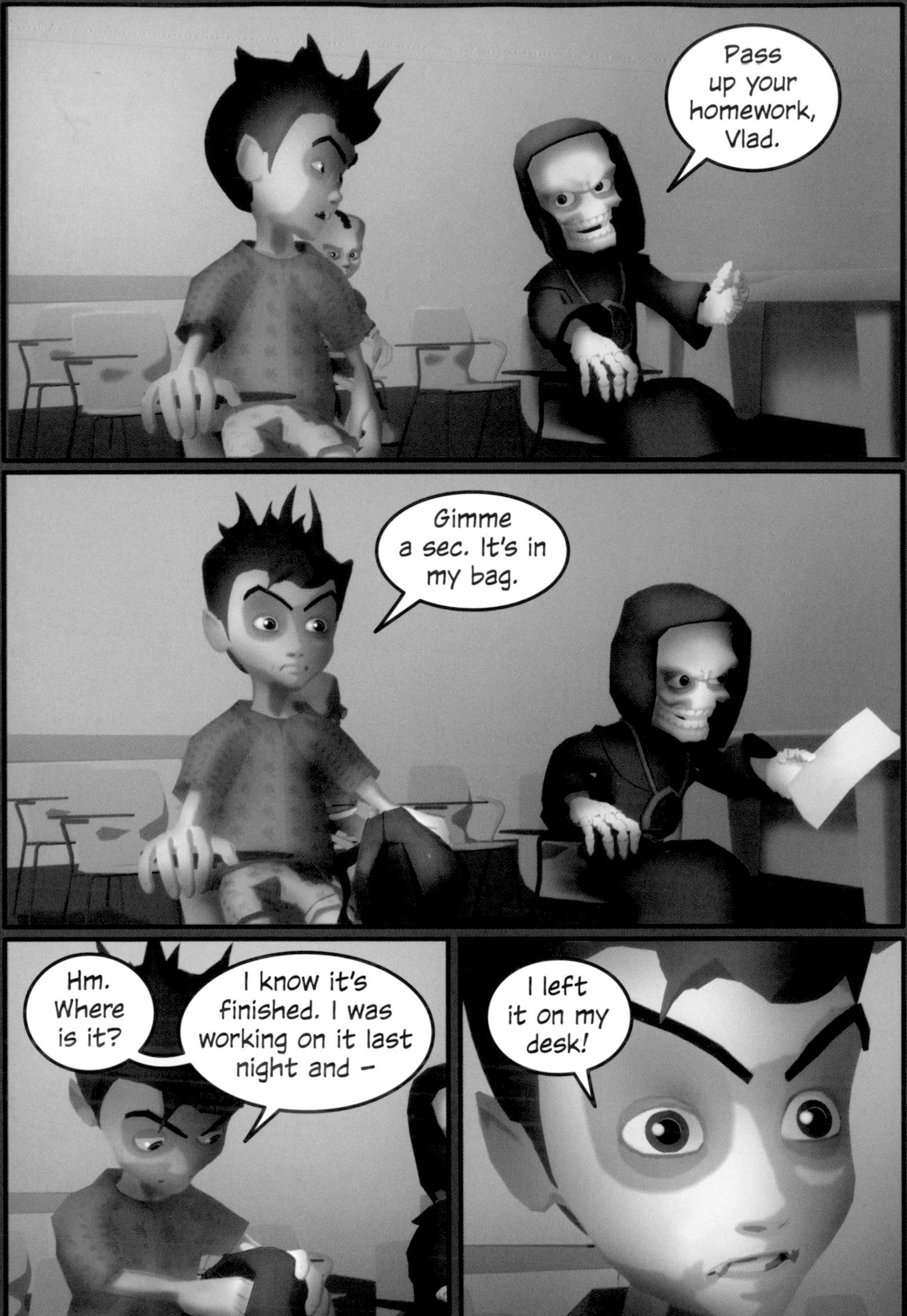
Pass up your homework, Vlad.
Gimme a sec. It's in my bag.
Hm. Where is it?
I know it's finished. I was working on it last night and –
I left it on my desk!

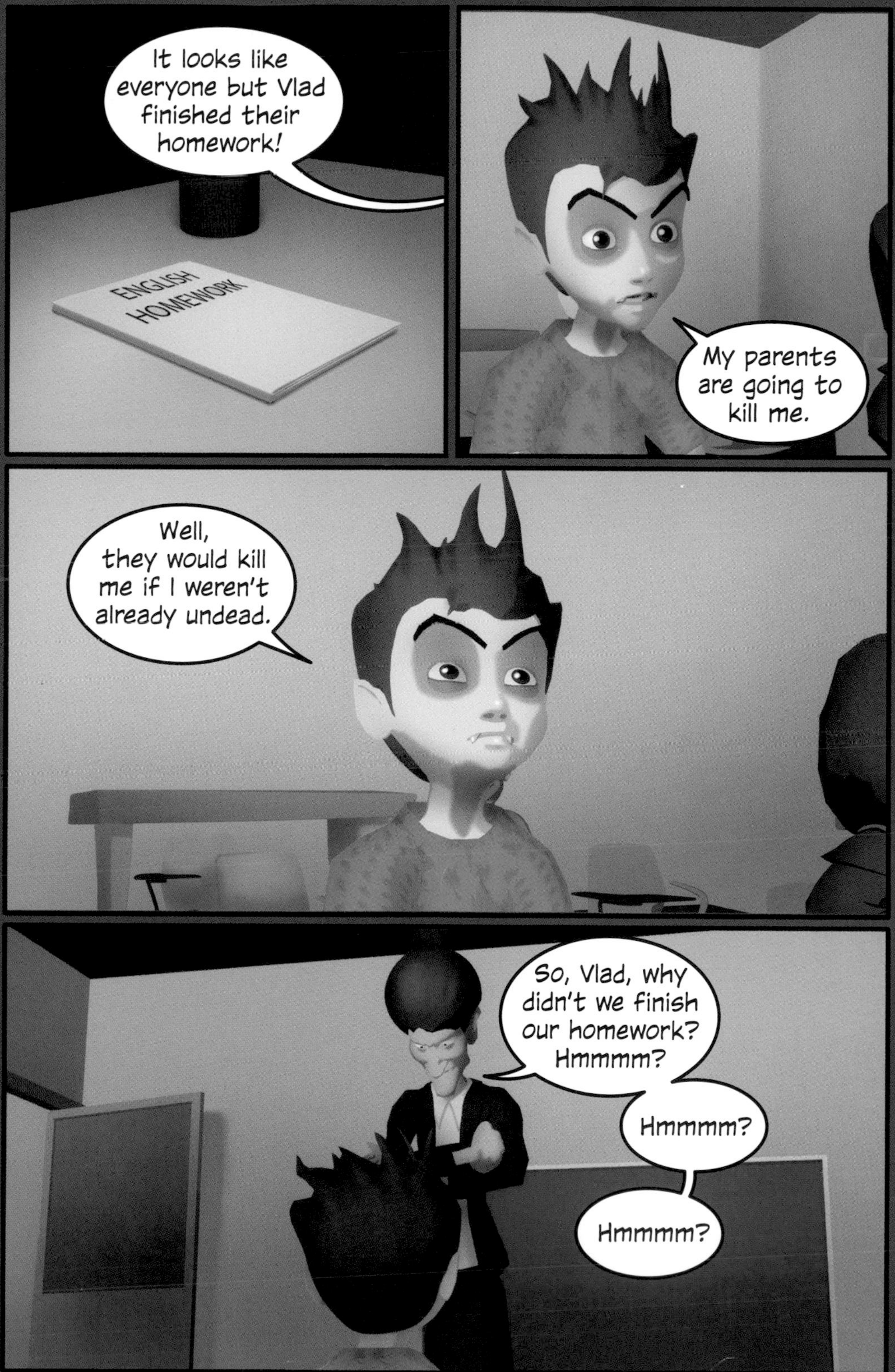
It looks like everyone but Vlad finished their homework!
ENGLISH HOMEWORK
My parents are going to kill me.
Well, they would kill me if I weren't already undead.
So, Vlad, why didn't we finish our homework? Hmmmm?
Hmmmm?
Hmmmm?

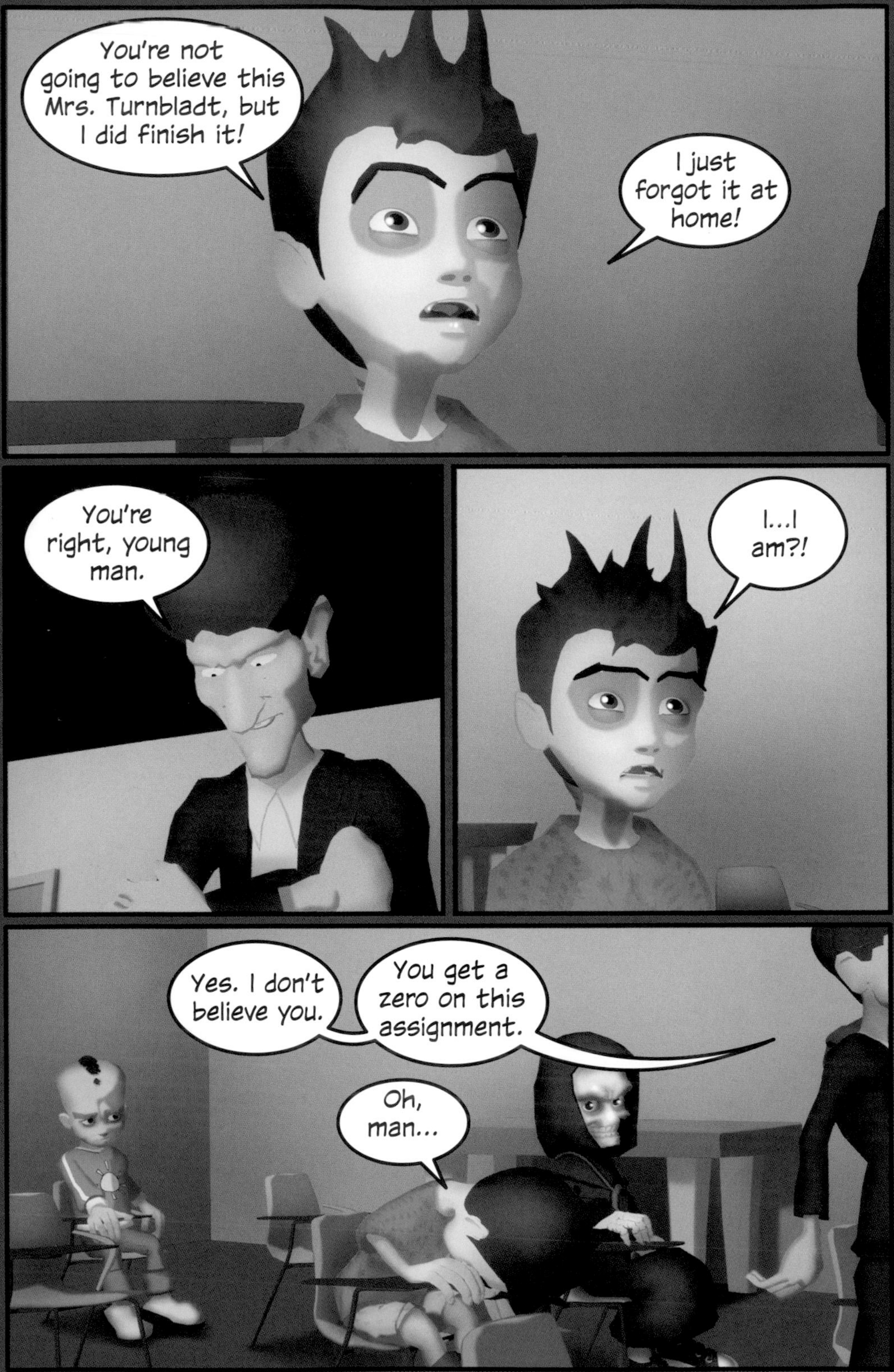
You're not going to believe this Mrs. Turnbladt, but I did finish it!
I just forgot it at home!
You're right, young man.
I...I am?!
Yes. I don't believe you.
You get a zero on this assignment.
Oh, man...

Later, in gym class . . .

Stretch it out, students. We're playing dodgeball today!

Is your day going any better now, Vlad?

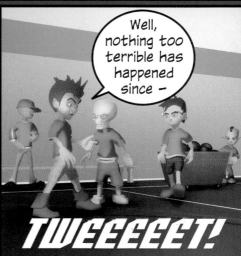

Well, nothing too terrible has happened since —

TWEEEEET!

THWACK!

Whoa!

That's gonna leave a mark.

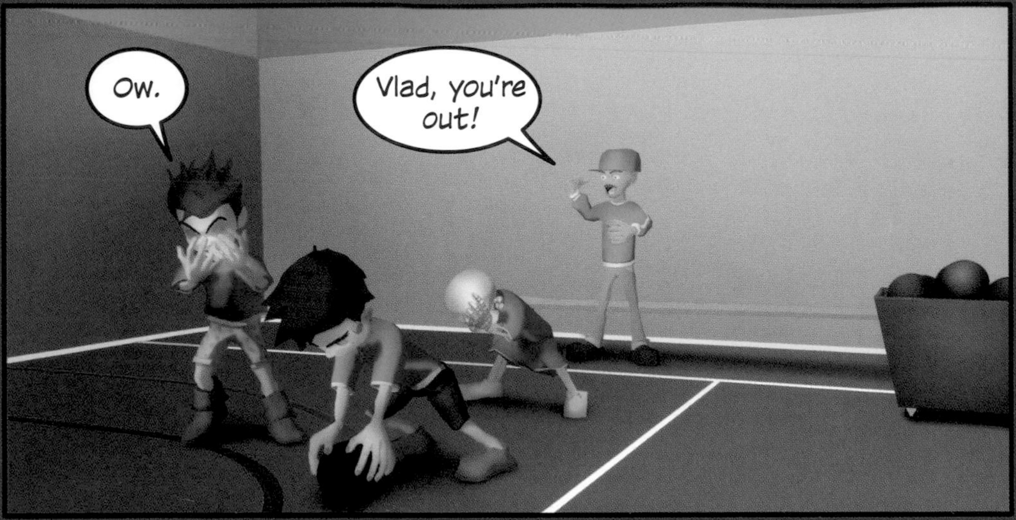
Ow.
Vlad, you're out!

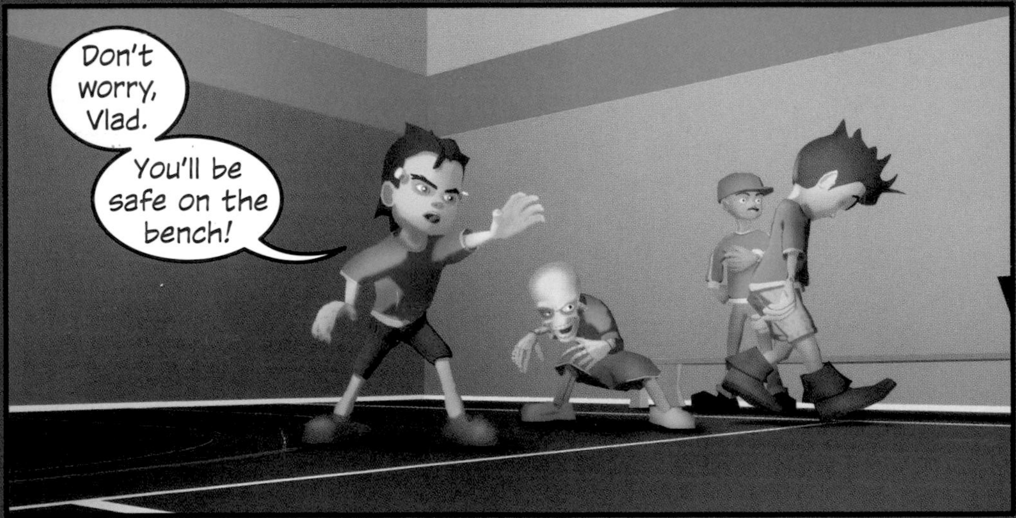
Don't worry, Vlad.
You'll be safe on the bench!

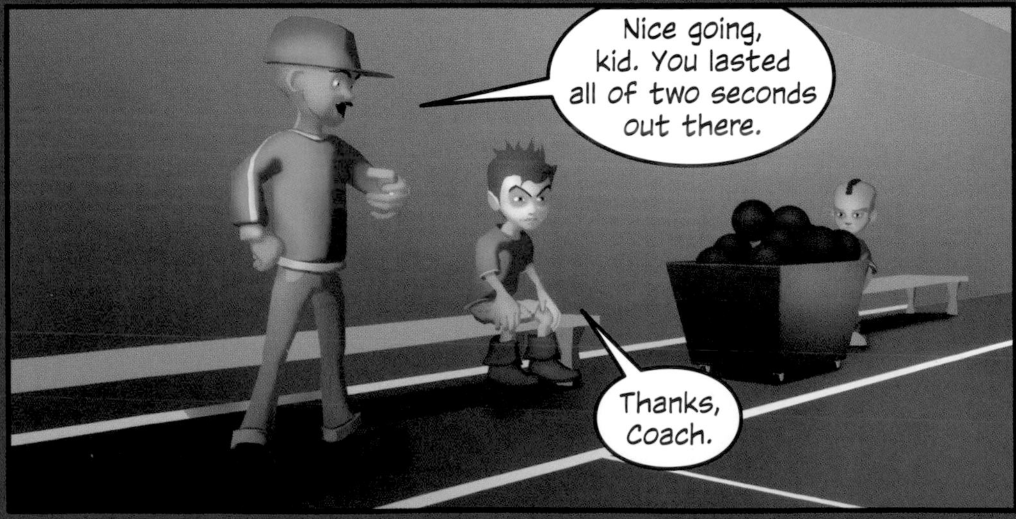
Nice going, kid. You lasted all of two seconds out there.
Thanks, Coach.

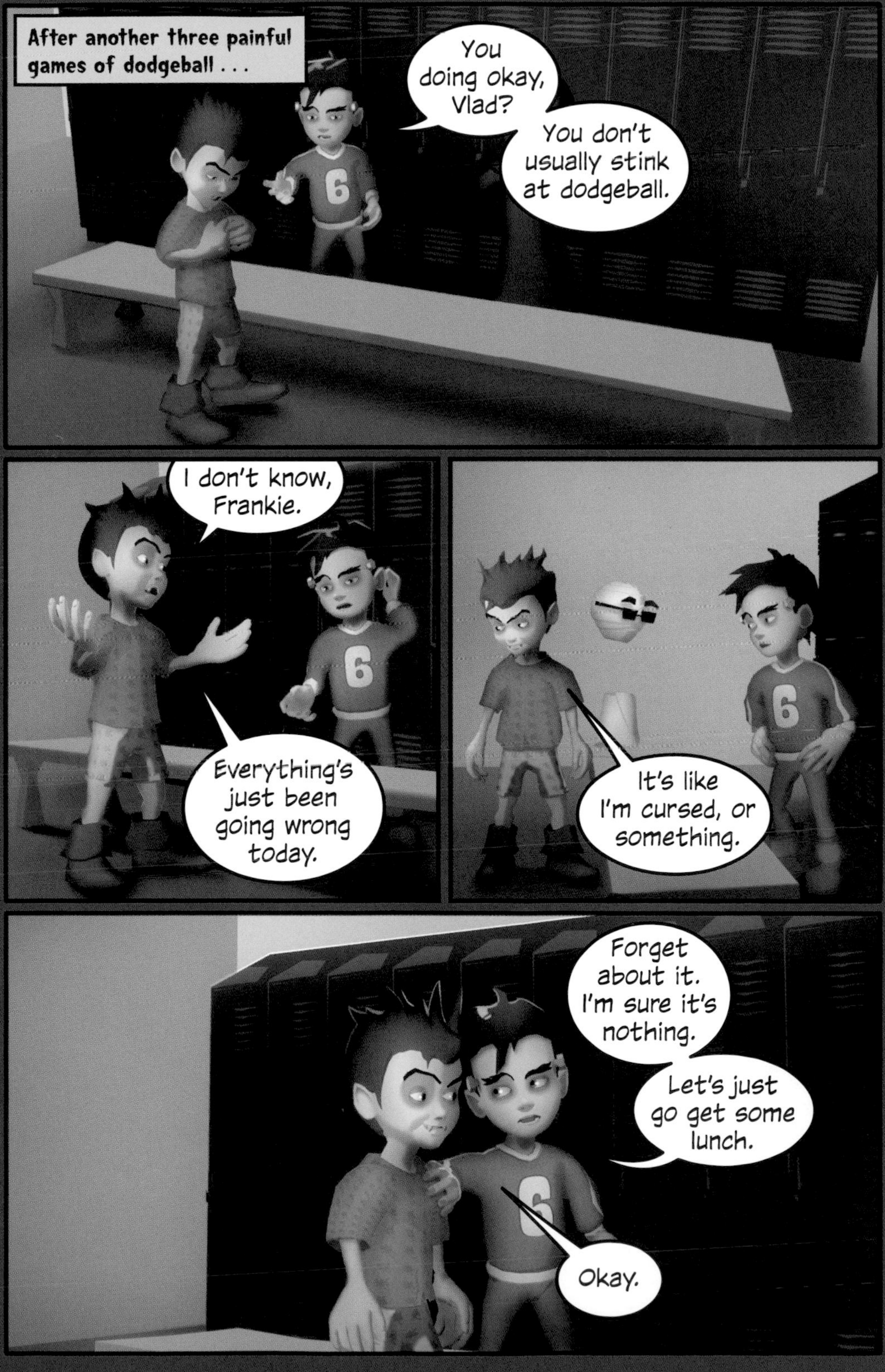
After another three painful games of dodgeball . . .
You doing okay, Vlad?
You don't usually stink at dodgeball.
I don't know, Frankie.
Everything's just been going wrong today.
It's like I'm cursed, or something.
Forget about it. I'm sure it's nothing.
Let's just go get some lunch.
Okay.

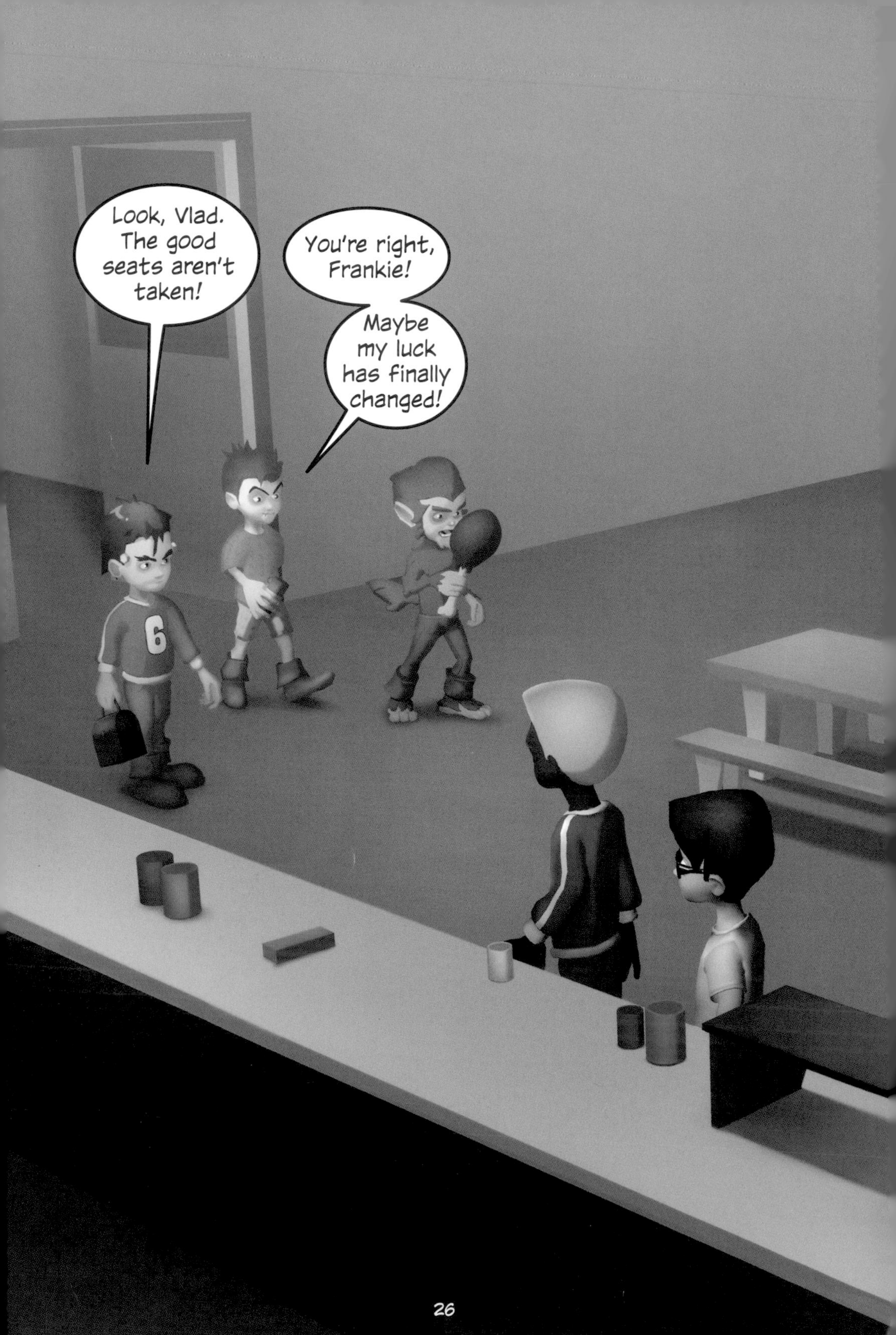
Look, Vlad. The good seats aren't taken!
You're right, Frankie!
Maybe my luck has finally changed!

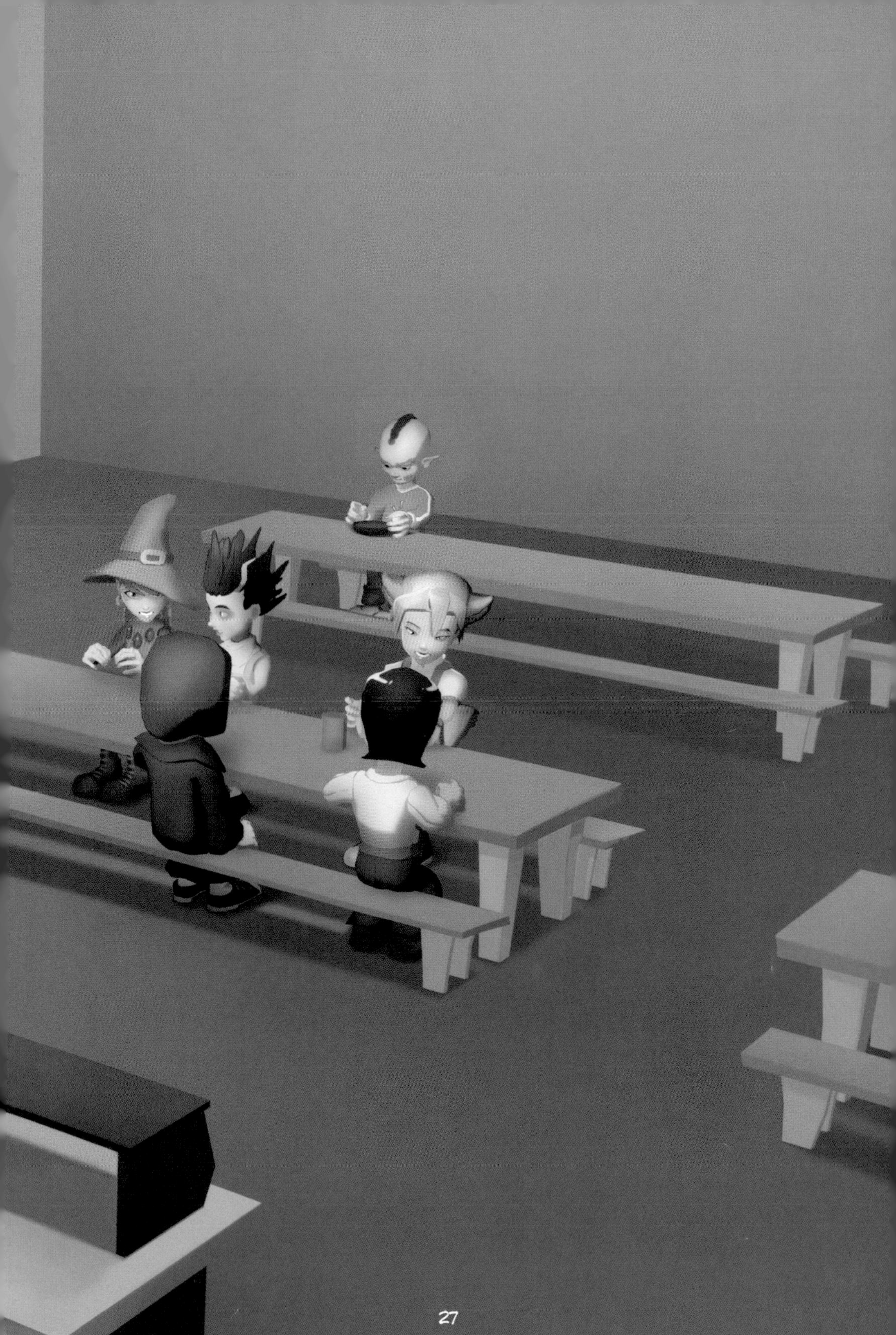

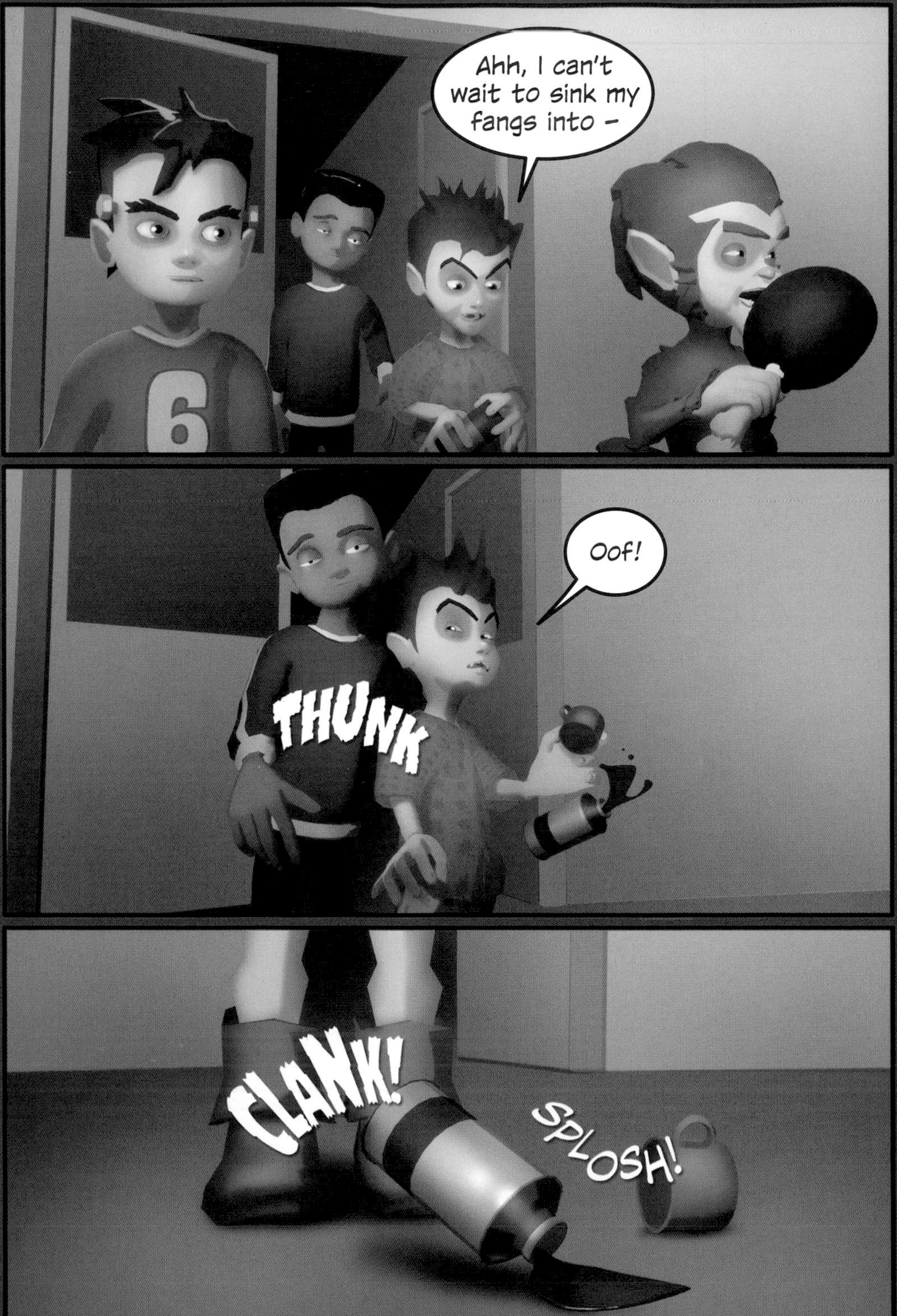
Ahh, I can't wait to sink my fangs into –
Oof!
THUNK
CLANK!
SPLOSH!

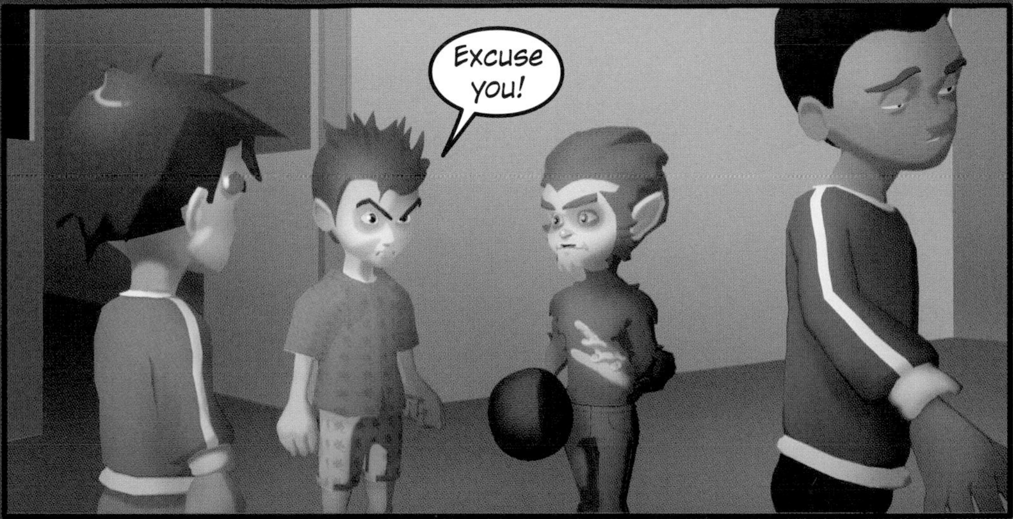
Excuse you!
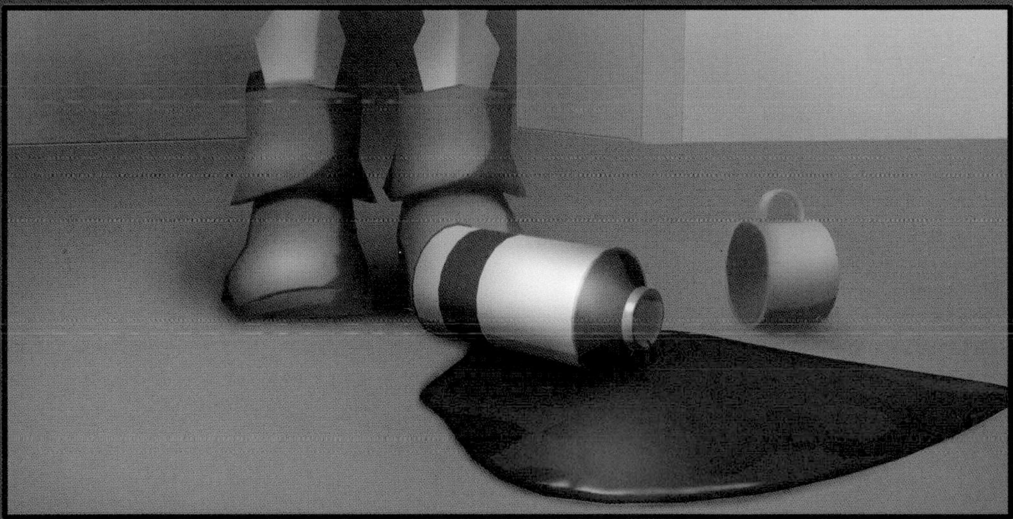
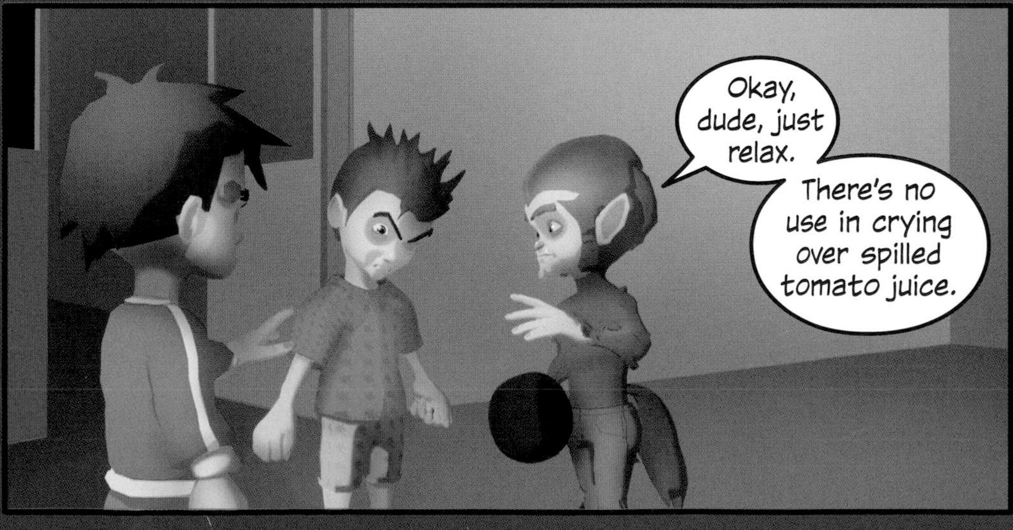
Okay, dude, just relax.
There's no use in crying over spilled tomato juice.

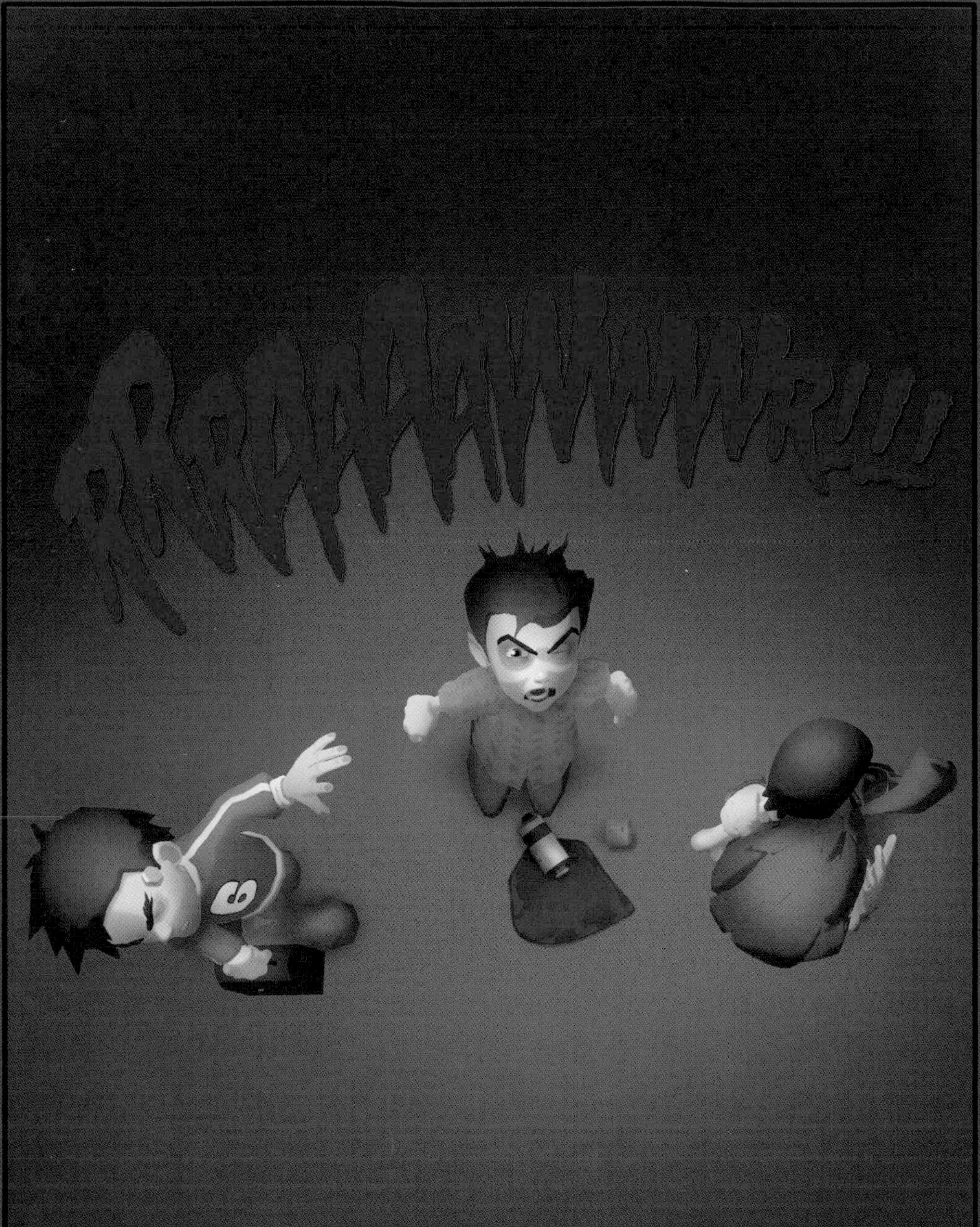
RRRAAAWWWWR!!!

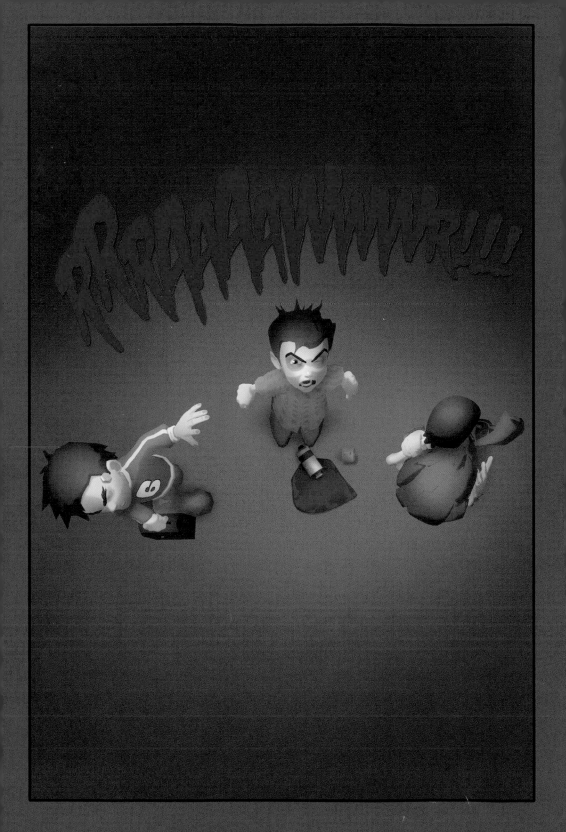

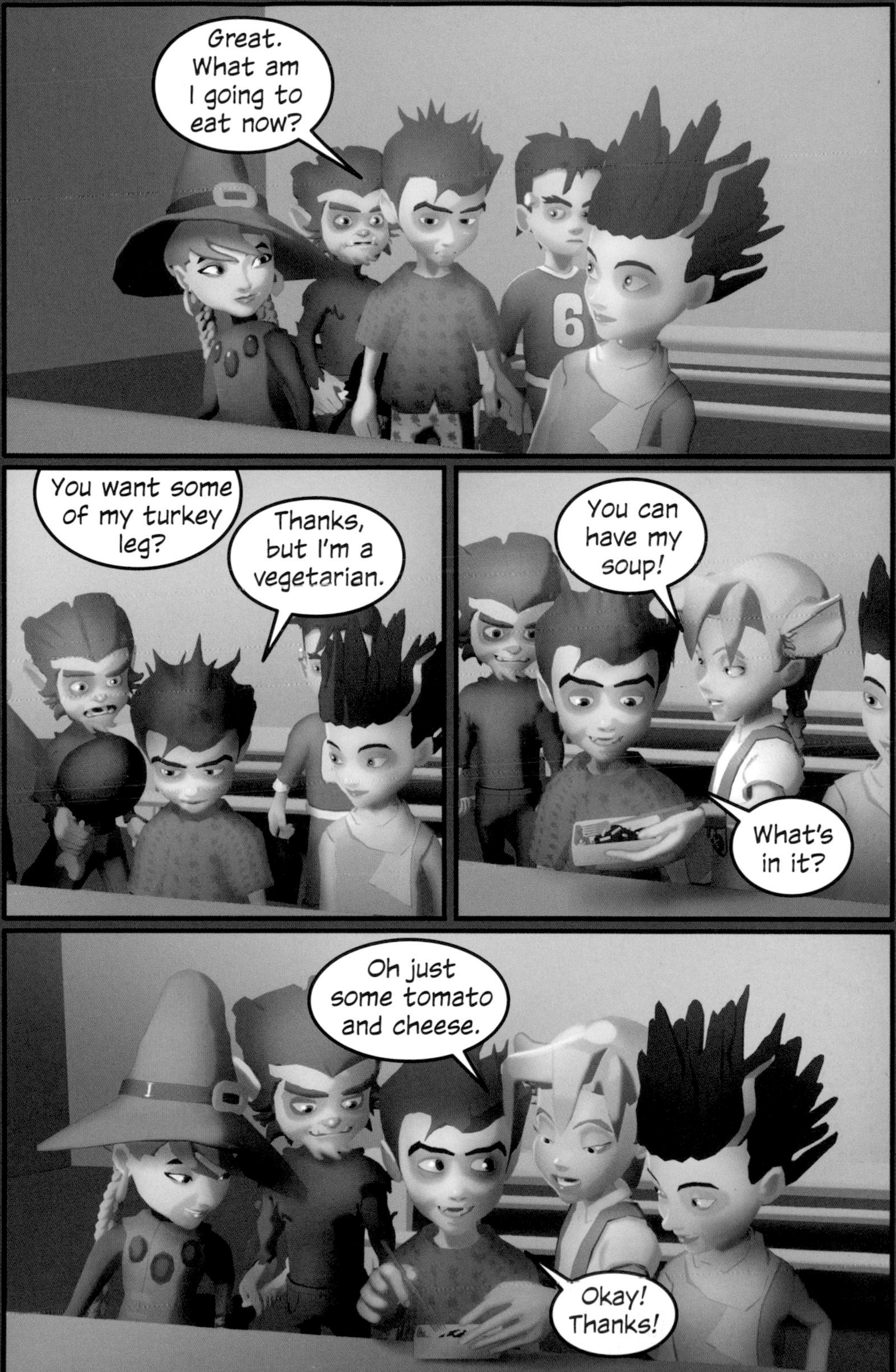
Great. What am I going to eat now?
You want some of my turkey leg?
Thanks, but I'm a vegetarian.
You can have my soup!
What's in it?
Oh just some tomato and cheese.
Okay! Thanks!

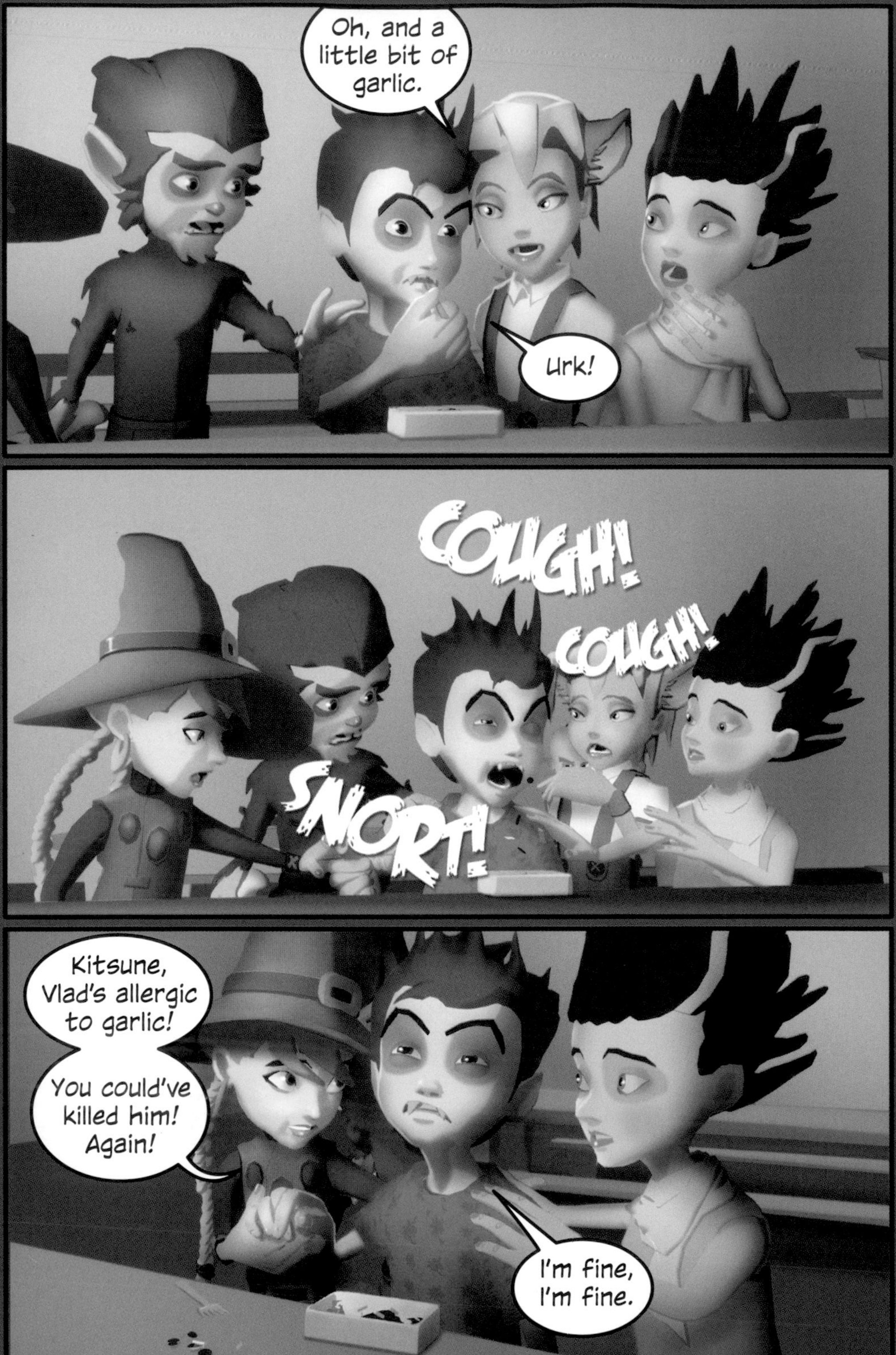
Oh, and a little bit of garlic.
Urk!
COUGH!
COUGH!
SNORT!
Kitsune, Vlad's allergic to garlic!
You could've killed him! Again!
I'm fine, I'm fine.

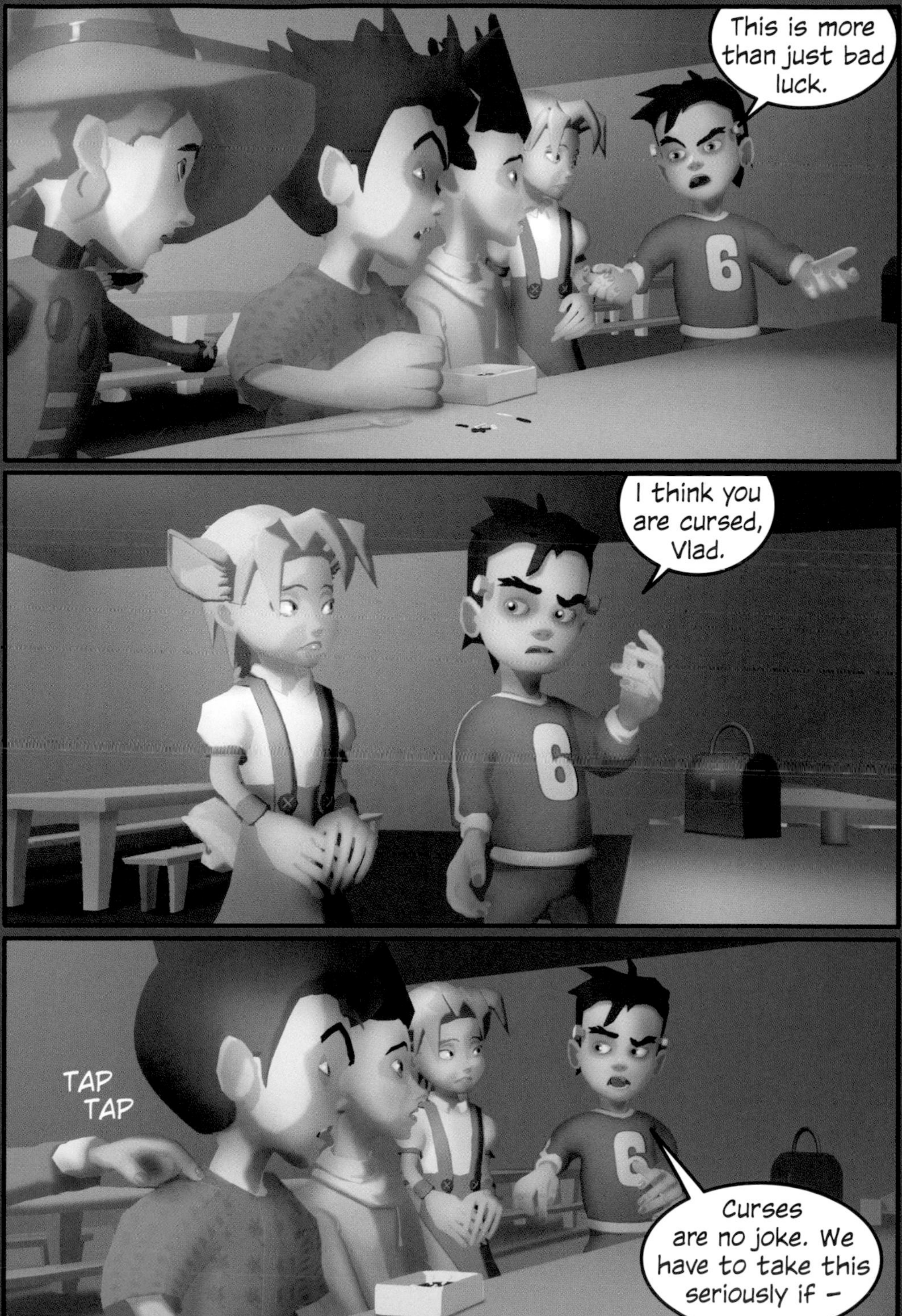
This is more than just bad luck.
I think you are cursed, Vlad.
TAP TAP
Curses are no joke. We have to take this seriously if –

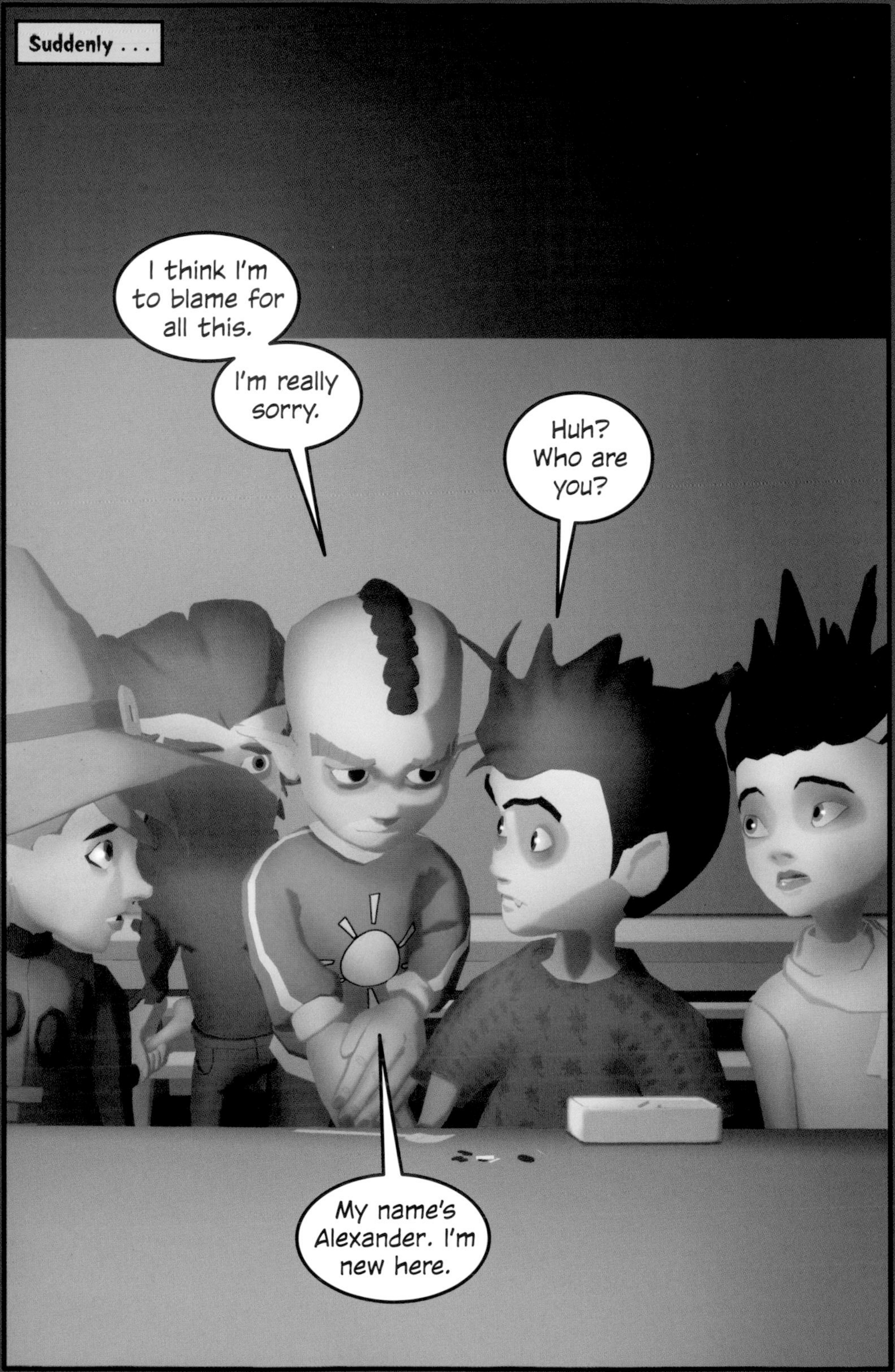
Suddenly . . .
I think I'm to blame for all this.
I'm really sorry.
Huh? Who are you?
My name's Alexander. I'm new here.

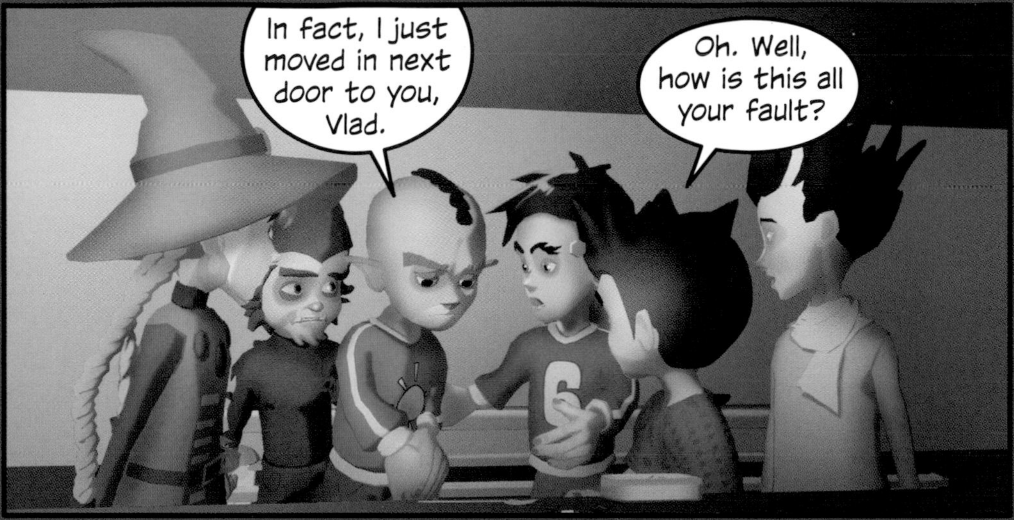
In fact, I just moved in next door to you, Vlad.
Oh. Well, how is this all your fault?

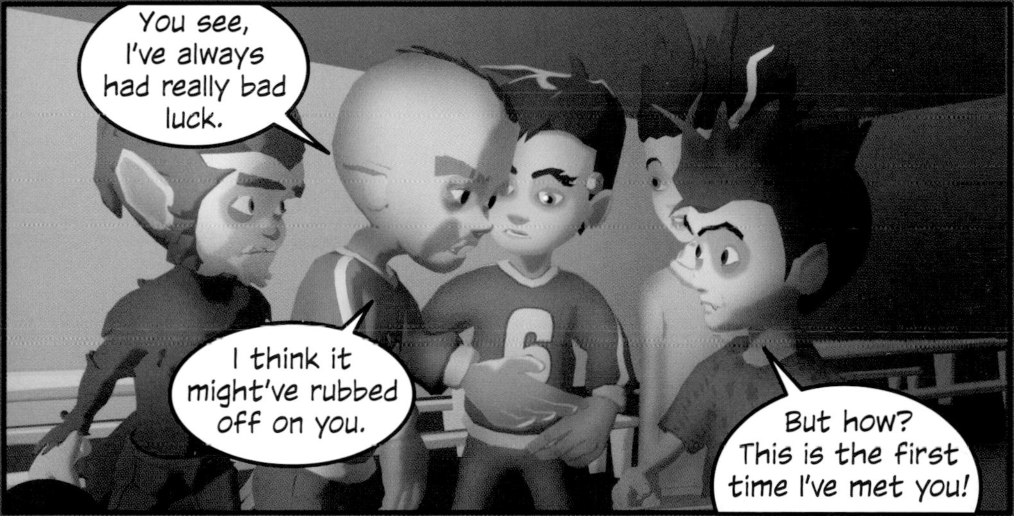
You see, I've always had really bad luck.
I think it might've rubbed off on you.
But how? This is the first time I've met you!

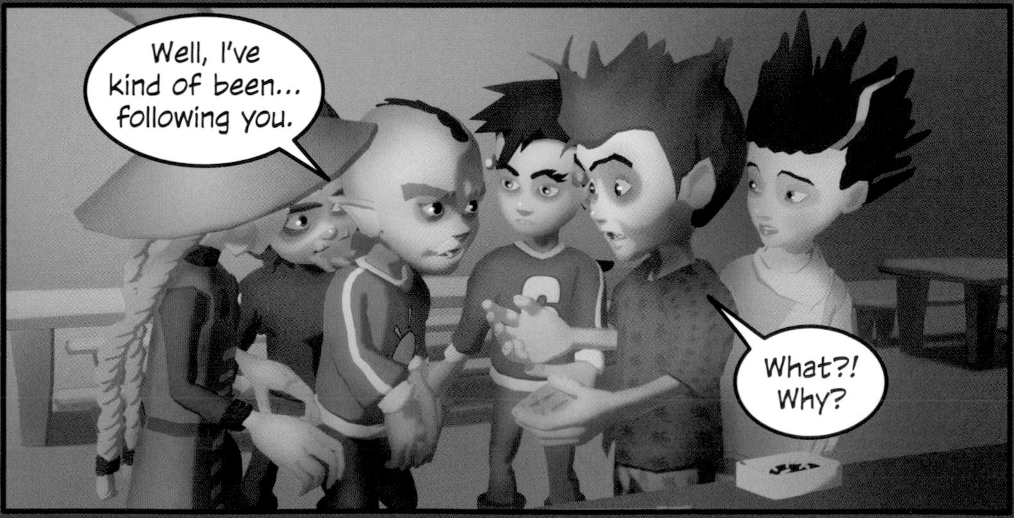
Well, I've kind of been... following you.
What?! Why?

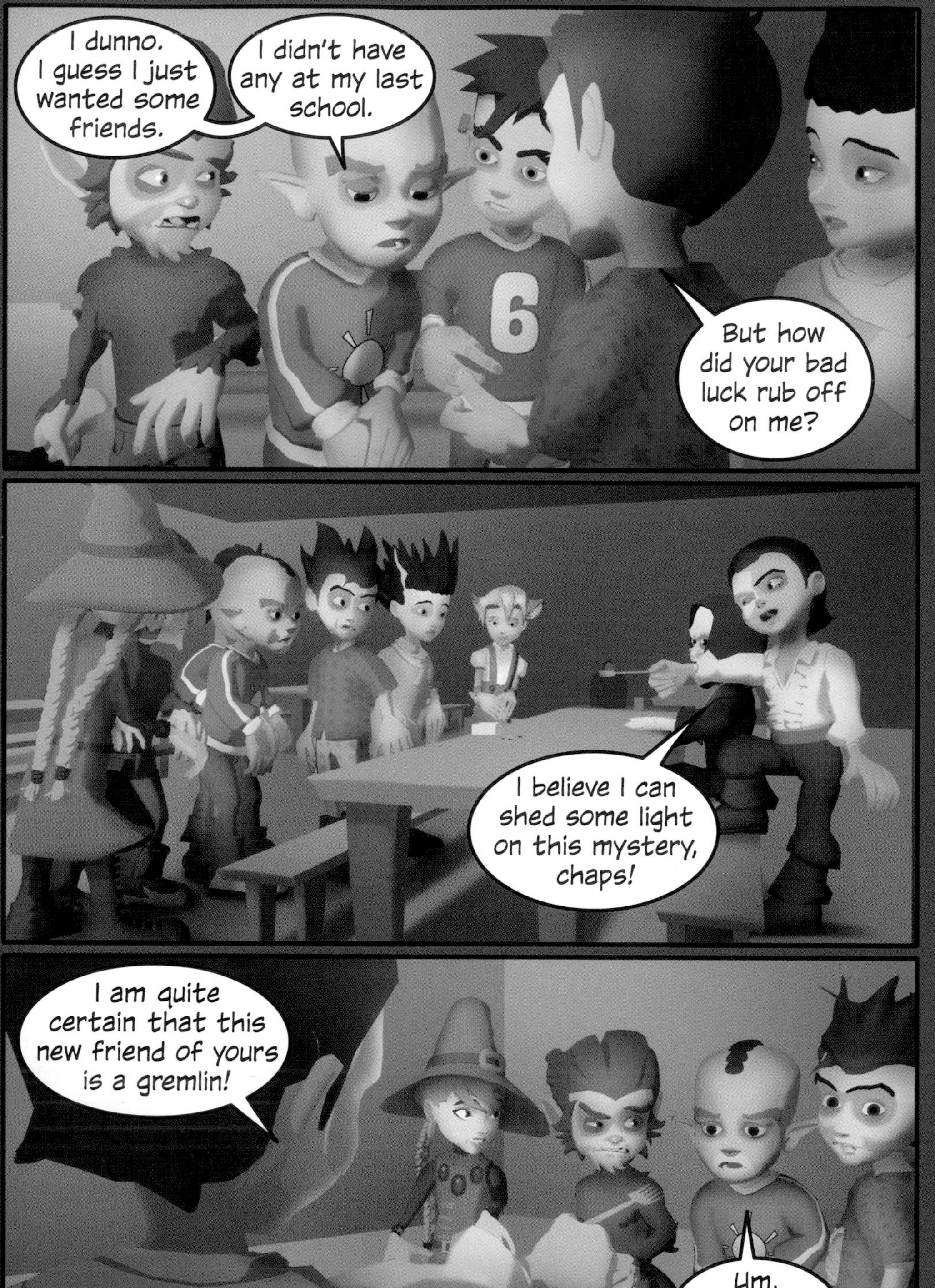
I dunno. I guess I just wanted some friends.
I didn't have any at my last school.
But how did your bad luck rub off on me?
I believe I can shed some light on this mystery, chaps!
I am quite certain that this new friend of yours is a gremlin!
Um, yeah, I am. So what?

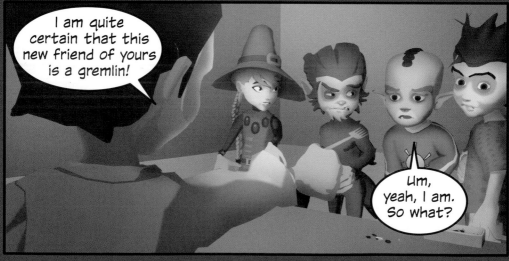

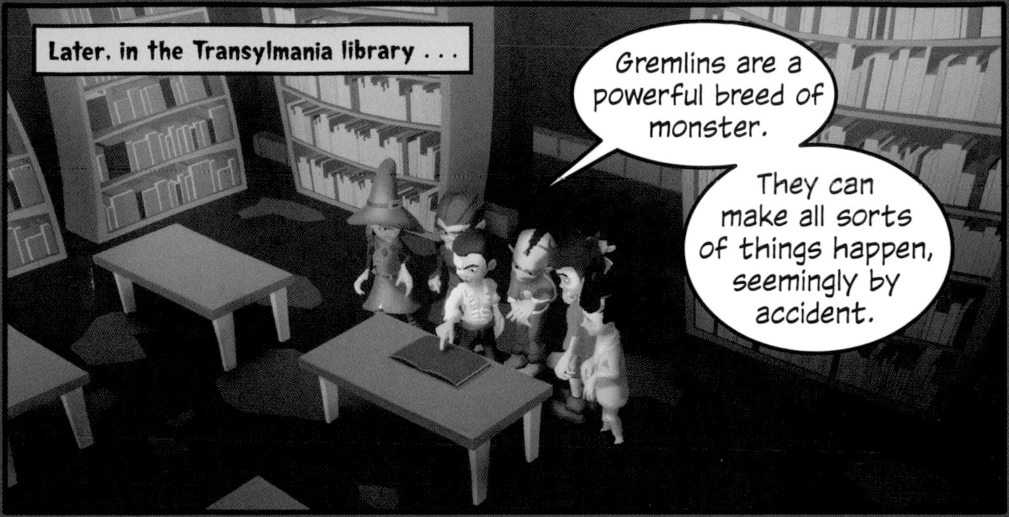
Later, in the Transylmania library . . .
Gremlins are a powerful breed of monster.
They can make all sorts of things happen, seemingly by accident.

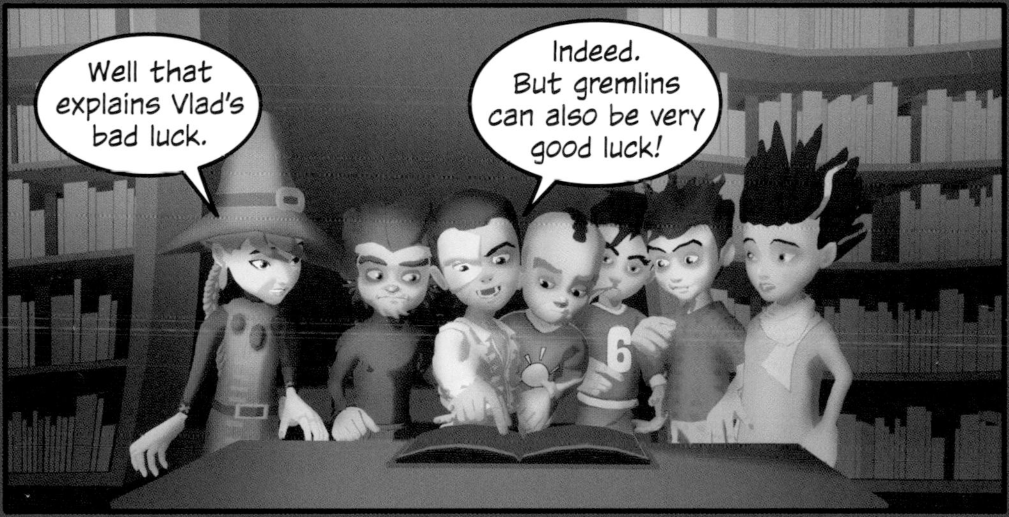
Well that explains Vlad's bad luck.
Indeed. But gremlins can also be very good luck!

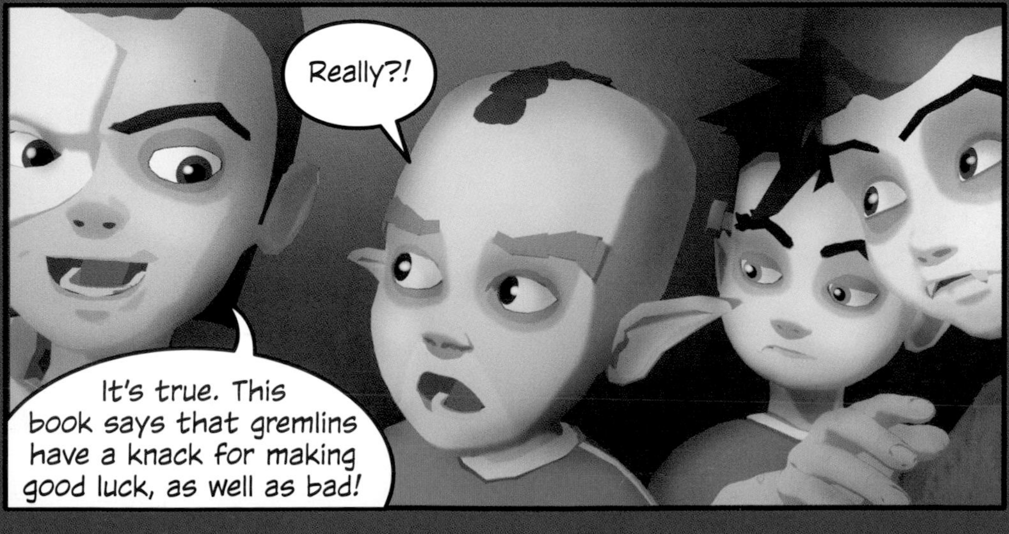
Really?!
It's true. This book says that gremlins have a knack for making good luck, as well as bad!

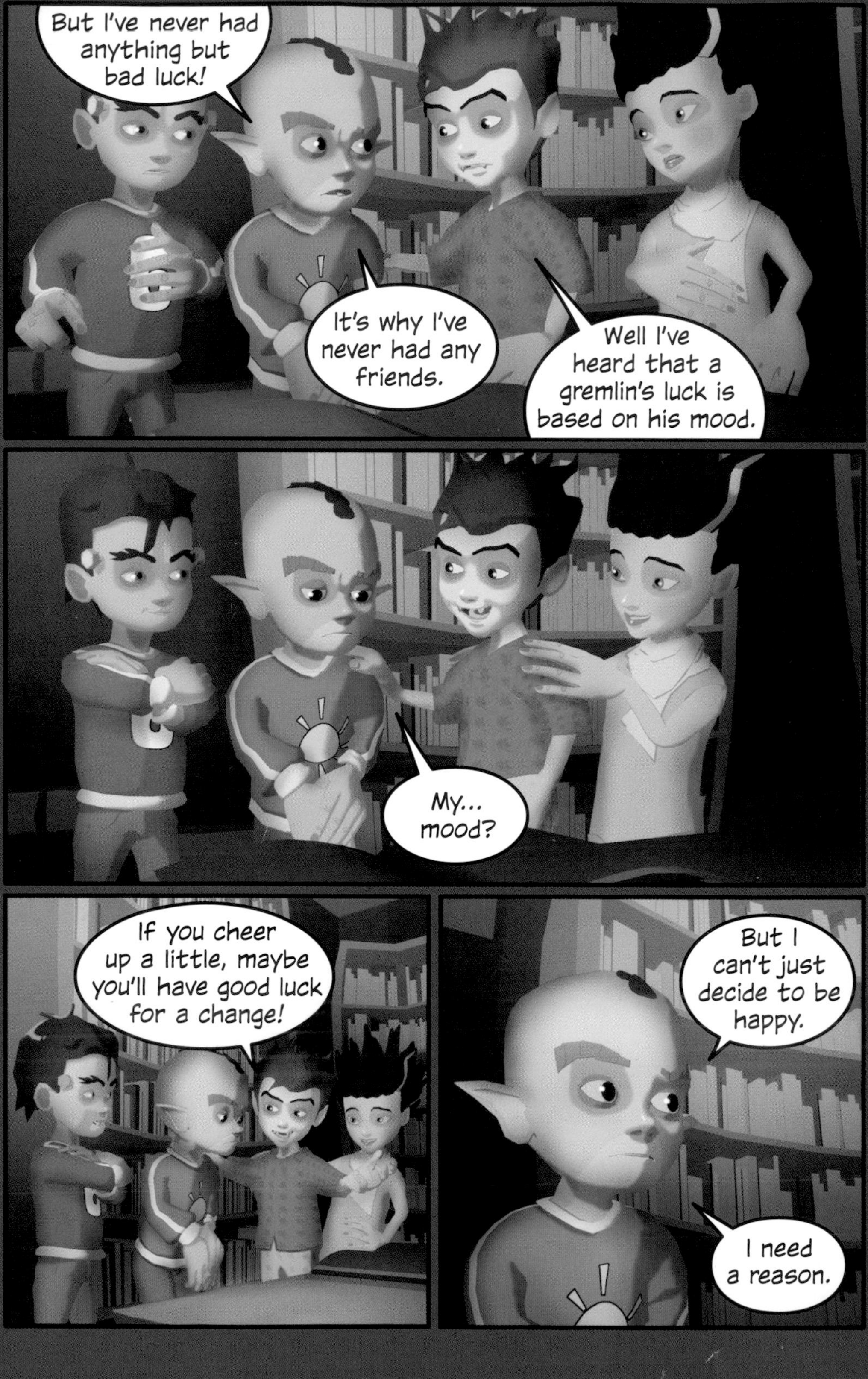
But I've never had anything but bad luck!
It's why I've never had any friends.
Well I've heard that a gremlin's luck is based on his mood.
My... mood?
If you cheer up a little, maybe you'll have good luck for a change!
But I can't just decide to be happy.
I need a reason.

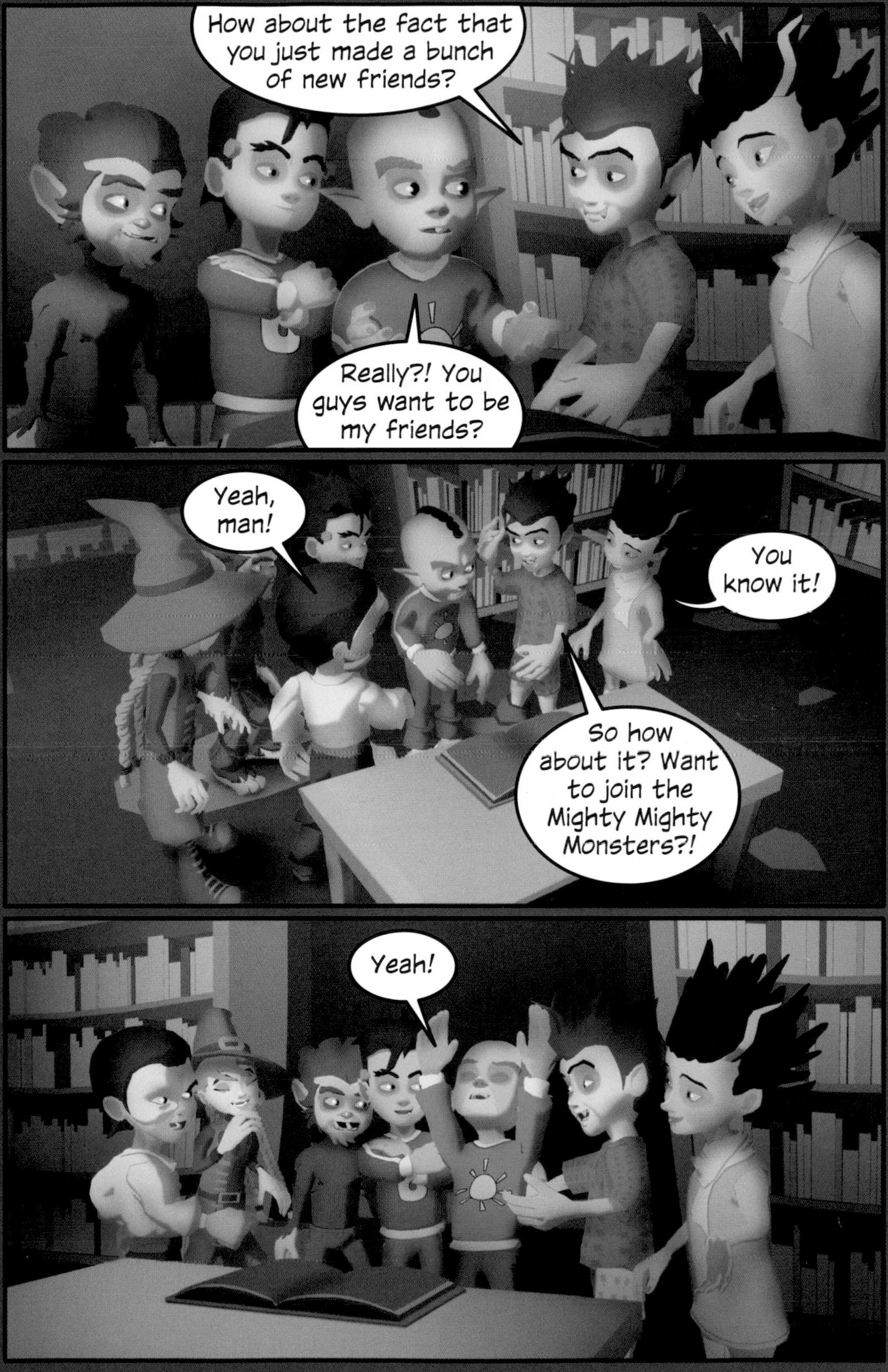
How about the fact that you just made a bunch of new friends?
Really?! You guys want to be my friends?
Yeah, man!
You know it!
So how about it? Want to join the Mighty Mighty Monsters?!
Yeah!

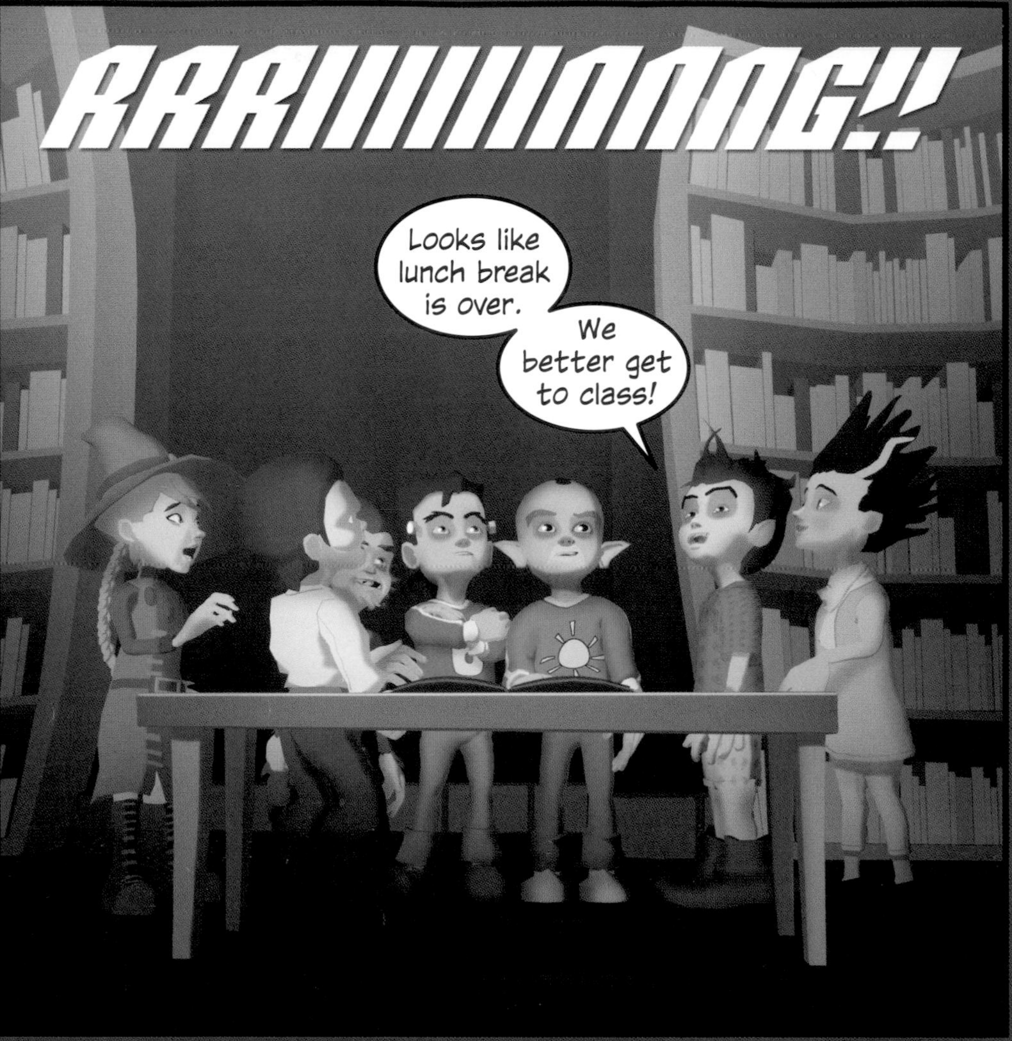
RRRIIIIIINNNG!!
Looks like lunch break is over.
We better get to class!

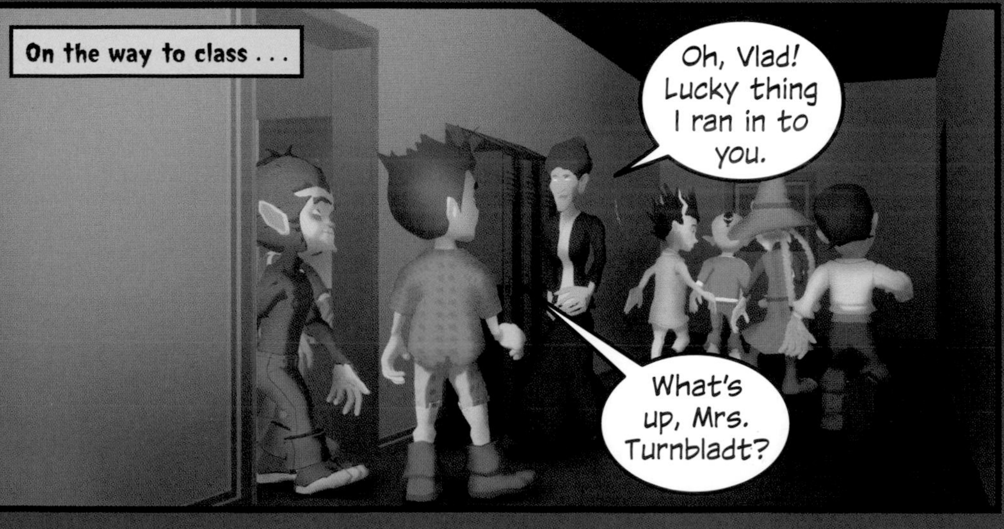
On the way to class . . .
Oh, Vlad! Lucky thing I ran in to you.
What's up, Mrs. Turnbladt?

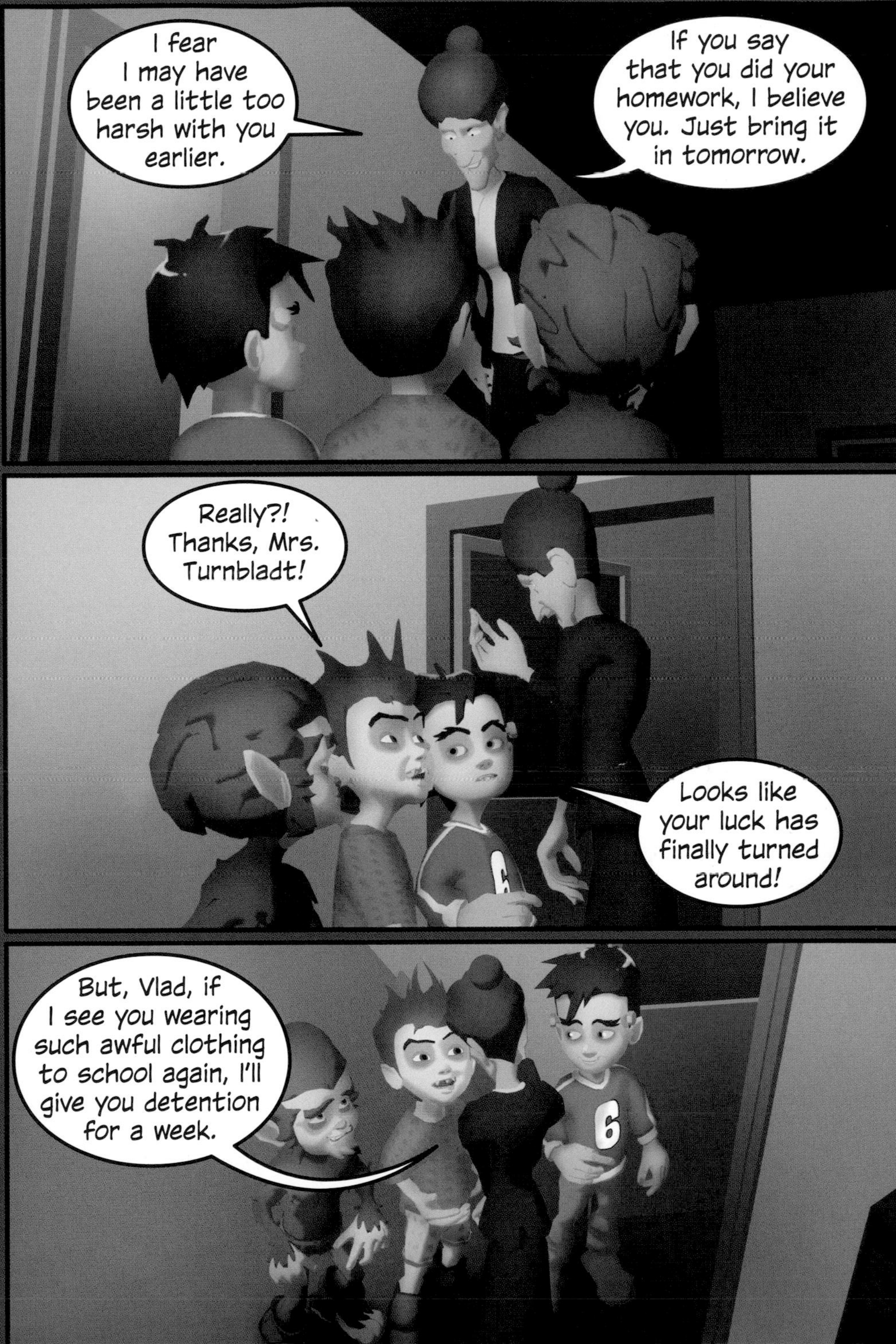
I fear I may have been a little too harsh with you earlier.
If you say that you did your homework, I believe you. Just bring it in tomorrow.
Really?! Thanks, Mrs. Turnbladt!
Looks like your luck has finally turned around!
But, Vlad, if I see you wearing such awful clothing to school again, I'll give you detention for a week.
6

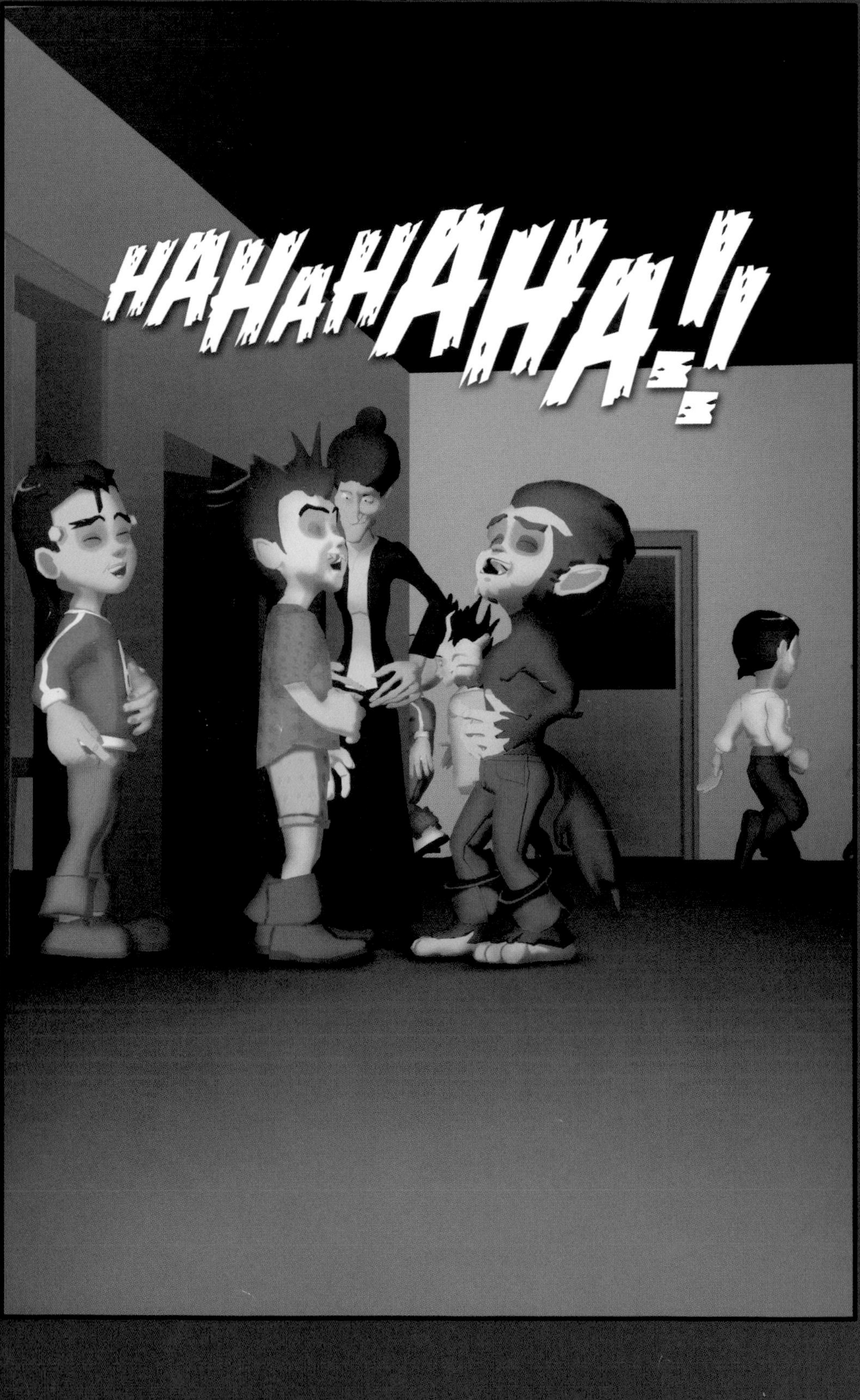
HAHAHAHAHA!!

ABOUT
SEAN O'REILLY
AND ARCANA STUDIO

As a lifelong comics fan, Sean O'Reilly dreamed of becoming a comic book creator. In 2004, he realized that dream by creating Arcana Studio. In one short year, O'Reilly took his studio from a one-person operation in his basement to an award-winning comic book publisher with more than 150 graphic novels produced for Harper Collins, Simon & Schuster, Random House, Scholastic, and others.

Within a year, the company won many awards including the Shuster Award for Outstanding Publisher and the Moonbeam Award for top children's graphic novel. O'Reilly also won the Top 40 Under 40 award from the city of Vancouver and authored The Clockwork Girl for Top Graphic Novel at Book Expo America in 2009. Currently, O'Reilly is one of the most prolific independent comic book writers in Canada. While showing no signs of slowing down in comics, he now writes screenplays and adapts his creations for the big screen.

GLOSSARY

aced (AYSSD)—got a perfect score

breed (BREED)—a particular type of animal

colorblind (KUHL-ur-blined)—if you are colorblind, you cannot see certain colors

curse (KURSS)—an evil spell

electrocuted (i-LEK-truh-kyoo-tid)—injured or killed by a severe electric shock

gremlin (GREM-lin)—a mischievous being that causes troubles for others

knack (NAK)—an ability to do something difficult or tricky

relax (ri-LAKS)—become less tense and anxious

typical (TIP-uh-kuhl)—normal, or in a usual way

undead (un-DED)—no longer alive, but instead animated by a supernatural force, like a vampire or zombie

vegetarian (vej-uh-TARE-ee-uhn)—someone who eats only plants

DISCUSSION QUESTIONS

1. Do you believe in good luck? How about bad luck? Why or why not?

2. Poto brings the other monsters to the library to find information about gremlins. When you go to the library, what do you look for? What are your favorite books? Talk about it.

3. Alexander struggles to find friends as the new kid in school. Have you ever been the new kid at school? What do you think it's like to not know anyone at your school? Talk about the challenges of being a new kid.

WRITING PROMPTS

1. Alexander the gremlin has trouble making friends. How many friends do you have? Do you wish you had more friends? Write about friendship.

2. Vlad has a bad hair day and has to wear mismatched clothing to school. What are some other embarrassing things that could happen to someone at school? Write about a student's really bad school day.

3. Ms. Turnbladt punishes Vlad for forgetting to bring his homework to school. Have you ever been punished for something in school? What happened? Write about it.

Mighty Mighty MONSTERS ADVENTURES

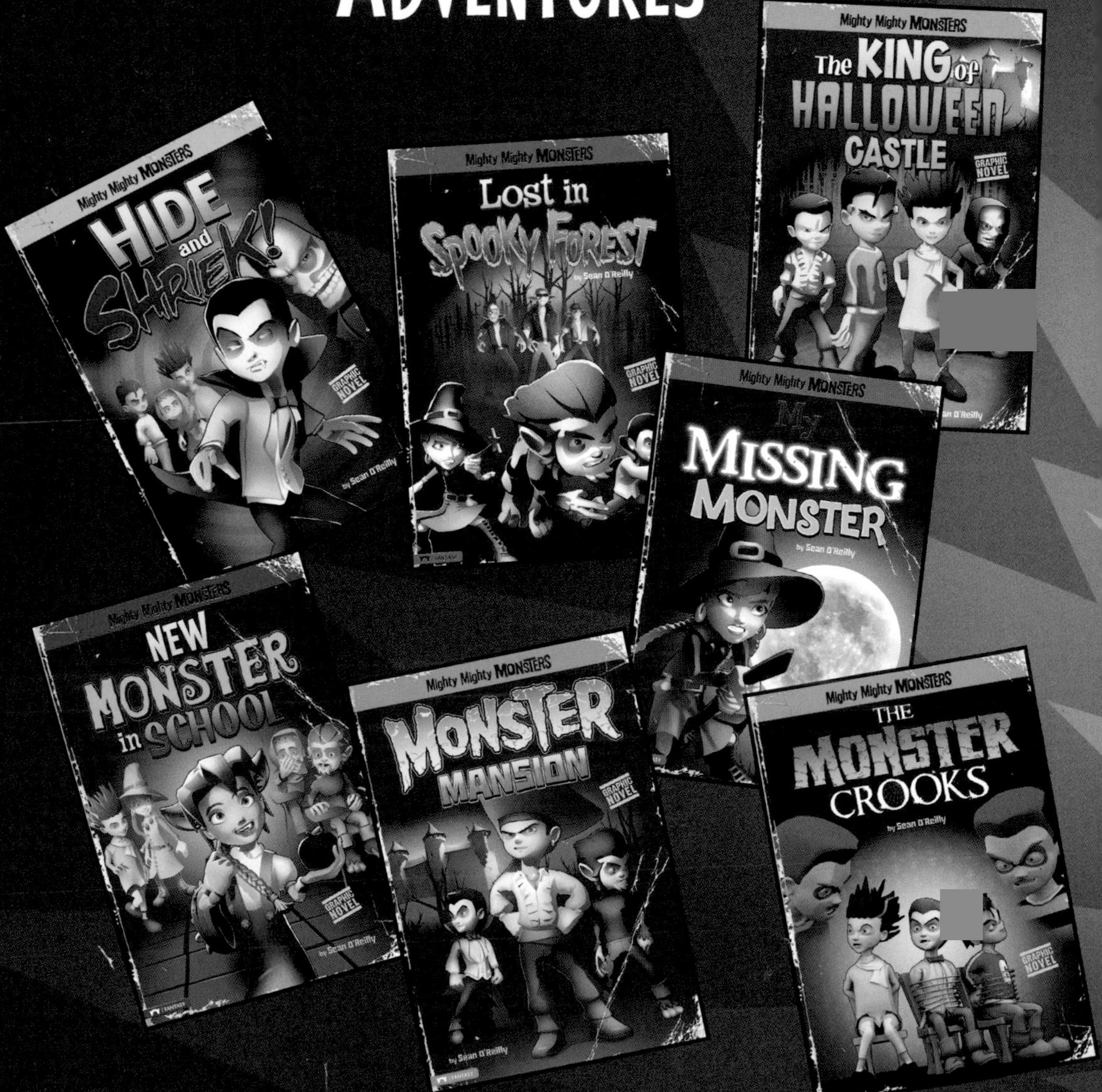
Mighty Mighty MONSTERS
The KING of HALLOWEEN CASTLE
GRAPHIC NOVEL
Mighty Mighty MONSTERS
HIDE and SHRIEK!
GRAPHIC NOVEL
by Sean O'Reilly
Mighty Mighty MONSTERS
Lost in Spooky Forest
by Sean O'Reilly
GRAPHIC NOVEL
Mighty Mighty MONSTERS
My Missing Monster
by Sean O'Reilly
Mighty Mighty MONSTERS
NEW MONSTER in SCHOOL
GRAPHIC NOVEL
by Sean O'Reilly
Mighty Mighty MONSTERS
MONSTER MANSION
GRAPHIC NOVEL
by Sean O'Reilly
Mighty Mighty MONSTERS
THE MONSTER CROOKS
by Sean O'Reilly
GRAPHIC NOVEL

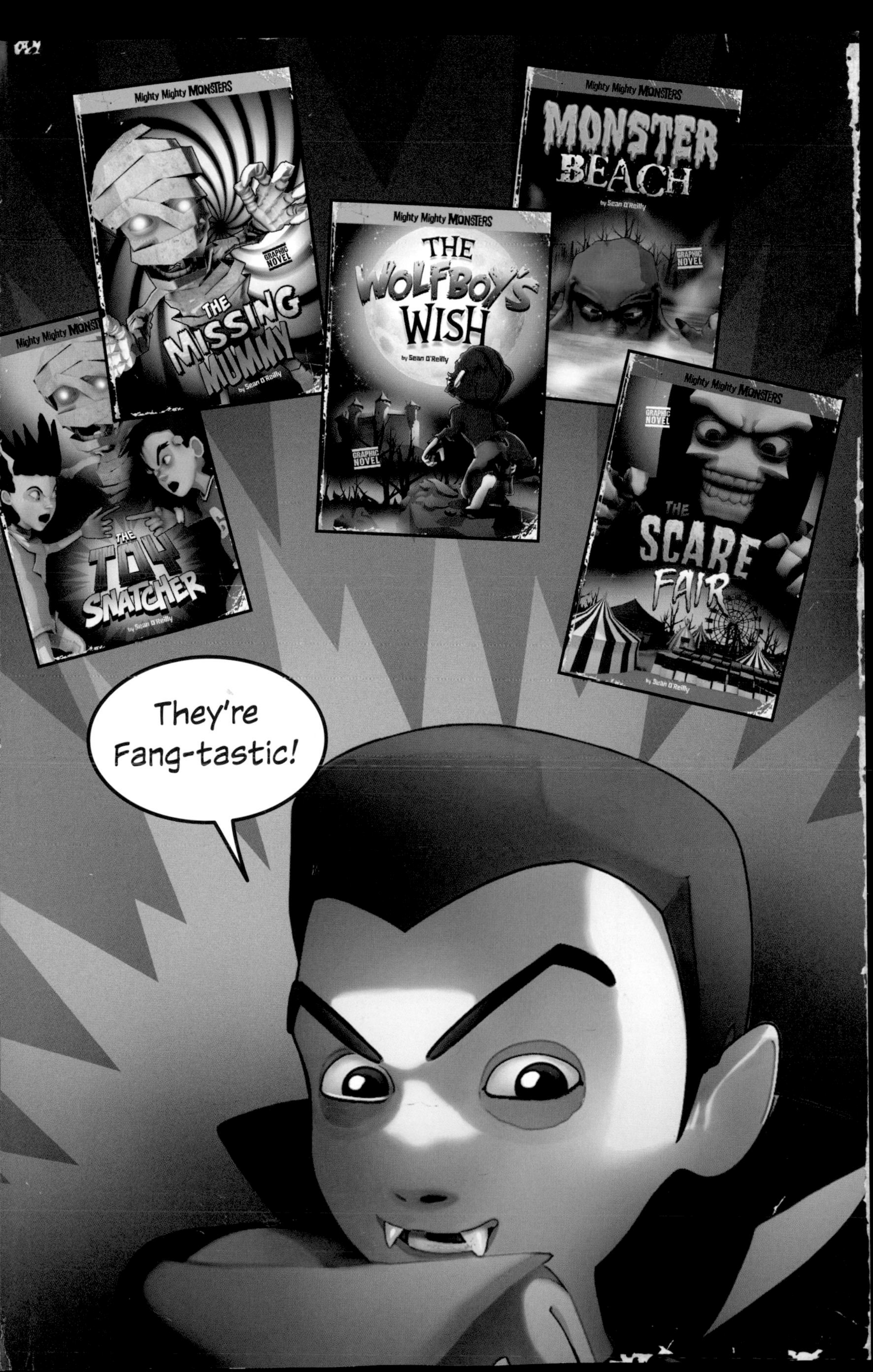
Mighty Mighty MONSTERS
THE MISSING MUMMY
by Sean O'Reilly
GRAPHIC NOVEL
Mighty Mighty MONSTERS
MONSTER BEACH
by Sean O'Reilly
GRAPHIC NOVEL
Mighty Mighty MONSTERS
THE WOLFBOY'S WISH
by Sean O'Reilly
GRAPHIC NOVEL
Mighty Mighty MONSTERS
THE TOY SNATCHER
by Sean O'Reilly
Mighty Mighty MONSTERS
GRAPHIC NOVEL
THE SCARE FAIR
by Sean O'Reilly
They're Fang-tastic!

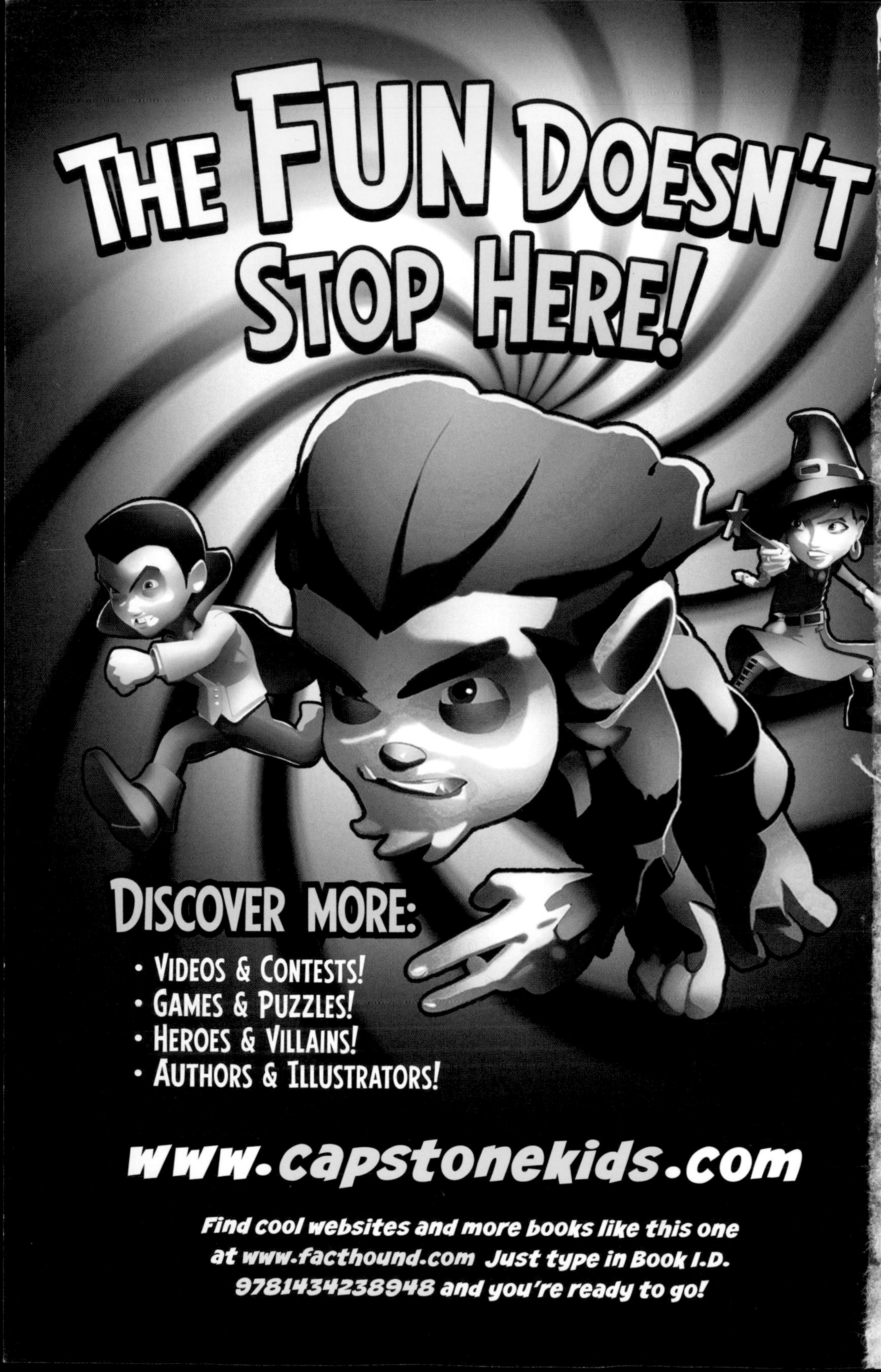
THE FUN DOESN'T STOP HERE!
DISCOVER MORE:
• VIDEOS & CONTESTS!
• GAMES & PUZZLES!
• HEROES & VILLAINS!
• AUTHORS & ILLUSTRATORS!
www.capstonekids.com
Find cool websites and more books like this one at www.facthound.com Just type in Book I.D. 9781434238948 and you're ready to go!